A Partial View Toward Nazareth

Kathryn Rantala

Published by Casa de Snapdragon Publishing LLC
A Traditional, Independent Publishing Company

Library of Congress Cataloging-in-Publication Data

Rantala, Kathryn.
A partial view toward Nazareth / Kathryn Rantala.
p. cm.
ISBN 978-0-9840530-9-4 (pbk.)
I. Title.
PS3618.A688P37 2010
811'.6--dc22

2010033011

20100831

Casa de Snapdragon Publishing LLC

Printed in the United States of America

Contents

Introduction

"Outpacing the Self"

(Any little thing is water. *Gertrude Stein, "Tender Buttons"*)

I know no author and poet writing today quite like Kathryn Rantala. Quirky, with an edge yet magical and melancholy, Kathryn has a sharp and clear style that surrounds everything that she writes. Like Marianne Moore, she is an inspired collector but Rantala depicts a more human scene. She is stoic yet she has heart. Norman lock has said that Rantala creates "a beautiful compression," unifying a fractured world. "Commonality is all." Reading her writing, I gain the distance I feel looking at a Chinese scroll. Where does she live? She lives not far from Palouse, reminiscent of Italy but, instead of vineyards, the Palouse produces wheat. It is a photographer's Mecca, a luminous landscape.

Rantala has written a book *Omnivory,* which describes her well. Her work has been called sublimely idiosyncratic and well-crafted. I was introduced to Rantala's work in *Archipelago.* The title suits since she is an island and a water person. Turned inward much of the time she puts down scenes with the accuracy of a mirror. The pieces are reflective yet steer clear of the hazard and monotony of confessional, self-referential poets.

When I learned that Kathryn has a Finnish background, I was not surprised that I heard the music of Sibelius, images of fjords and glacial moraines in her writing. I saw many hues of blue and teal greens. As in a Chinese scroll, the human figure almost disappears; the land is so much greater than the self. She portrays a wanderer who hopes to retrieve herself before her own winter sets in.

. . .wet reflections always turned her inward. Here, in these vast rolling fields, a part of herself wanders out of sight. She hopes to retrieve it before the snow.

Although Rantala is deeply connected with seasons, she lives in a time outside clock time.

We call our time a day. We stay all that day and the next, as possible as birds, our hands opening and closing on captive air.

Her work defies simple category (prose-poems may come closest.) She writes with a longing for something she cannot name. She sees both with the discerning eye of a scientist, and a lover's ardent eye.

I wanted something else (I always wanted something) and thought the black-edged sinew that circled the koi pond and held in the water might contain it. In the center (it was a large pond) I noticed an island the shape of Pohnpei. Micronesia was there whenever it was wanted though I was not precisely sure how it had gotten there—its arrangements of flowing, close leaves, its rocks and ferns and elevations.... I would have known it anywhere.

"The Statuary Garden."

~

A particular anger helped move the ground I worked in, the soil in which bulbs would be buried inches down—some of them dropped hastily because the digger is cold . . .

Thus *A Partial View Toward Nazareth,* begins. It is divided into five sections: "The Statuary Garden," "Lost Secrets of Meteorology," "The Jewel Encrusted Alligator," "A Partial View Toward Nazareth," and "In the Canopy." The view is *toward,* the glimpse *partial,* and Nazareth itself is neither named nor described outside the title. She is taking a pilgrimage toward Nazareth at an oblique angle toward the town which is the center of pilgrimage. There is nothing religious in this book but there is much which is reverential. The first image we are given is of her digging. These convey the particular human sphere in which Rantala breathes. There is a digger. There are bulbs being planted. Bulbs are to recur.

~

A partial view suggests the mystery of the whole. Rantala hovers on the borderline between mystery and the known. She wants to step a bit outside the body like the mystic. Never in a rush, she is like a pond rippled with a summer breeze. She is taking a pilgrimage toward a city not named in the book. Spiritually, her journey is a riff on the center of Christian pilgrimage.

~

After planting bulbs, she scrubs and goes out, no longer

looking inward. She wanders into a bookstore and examines a book with a plant leaf bookmark: *"It was green, embossed and clearly well cared for. Inside someone had pressed a large leaf against the cover—maybe madrona, but pretty wide for madrona, maybe rubber tree."* She is a gatherer, but not a hunter.

Back from her stroll, she lays her purchase on a table" *certain no angel would want a chair but might agree to lie in profile on a round, small, wooden surface happy to have a being on it shaped in a kind of S."*

This shows another of the poet's charms. Her eye can imagine an angel wanting to claim a chair or appear in profile (as angels often do in art) on a circular table content to be in the rather seductive posture of an "S."

Later, she describes JMW Turner:

More secretive than anyone, JMW Turner had a strong instinct for painting as performance and was generally one of the first to arrive at the Royal Academy, coming down before breakfast and continuing his labor as long as daylight lasted.

She is engaged another day by De Chirico. She *"was distracted by the De Chirico print, L'Angoisse du depart—a thing so confident of itself it could have chosen to hang anywhere. I don't know why it feels like that or why it would select this place and why looking at it, though it was thrilling, also made me think about the bulbs and what I had done to them. Asleep, dead, alive.... Who was I to say they must be everything?"*

The world she reflects is replete with such disparate things as a Steinway piano, second hand bookstore, and a "jewel-encrusted alligator." Her world is lapidary, her voice intimate: "in the answering way of conversation." The imaginary compels. "It is the imaginary Appaloosa that inspires. My homing instinct is strong and moody."

Rantala could be called a Victorian. But not for long. She is a modern whose language is contemporary, whose precision is watermark. "Hunching is not allowed."

One of her several secrets is being both personal and impersonal; I find her voice both intimate and distanced.

I have found one elegy in the book, "The Mango Pots of Verve." The inclusion of the "widow" in the title and parenthesized evokes her late husband with control, quiet, understatement.

The Mango Pots of *Veuve* *(The Widow) Rantala*

The spider has for circuit, foreshortened.

Webbed mangoes,
crushed considerations of flush trees.

Everyday like this

pots abiding the abodes of hiss

strange champagnes
drown the lucky snake
in his.

Everyday a beading rain.

Whether dealing with traffic patterns, statuary gardens,

or lost secrets of meteorology, Rantala is bent upon uncovering and discovering secrets. When she *re*covers the things seemingly lost, she wins thru to a wise, calm knowing that yet still is not satisfied. The secret of the spell she casts is that all these things in the final tableau, or call it mosaic, are placed in such an order that the work glows and moves us emotionally.

The music and the art she reflects upon are key.

She selects the precise piece of music to go with weather and time of day. Studying a print reminiscent of Thompson, she considers the world, which the print evokes. When her own house is buried in snow, she decides to marry this mood with music. She selects a Claudio Arrau version of Chopin *Nocturnes & Interludes*

In "Notes on Meditation" she writes:

He imagines there was music then, swelling toward him as nourishment, and shapes forming from angles and air. He believes that when he first opened his eyes he saw only blue and green, as cats do.

I asked Kathryn who her favorite composers are, and I also asked where she grew up:

"Bach and Rameau. I was born in Seattle and grew up in a house built by a ferry boat captain who modeled the rooms, doors, windows (portholes) after a ship."

Her musical meditations sustain. "No musical sound is isolate but is accompanied by harmonics."

It all figures: pieces fit like fine grooved pieces in a cabin. Nothing endures without change. If we cannot be wholly free, and we are all in part captive, we can be armed. Kathryn Rantala arms herself with minute observation, rapport with earth, the arts, and roots, her history.

This is a book, which I will keep opening. Rantala write of lost things such as "Aunt Rose's coin purse, Uncle Red's ring. The dead will have their writes."

I will come to this book in all seasons but perhaps most often in winter when the outer world is minimal, most spare. Captives, we all are. Yet we are all raptors as well. In blues and greens, I see a reflective, part melancholy, part reverential world. Listen to the rapture here:

When a moon change happens, when there is a rustle of any kind—a settle of hair, a brightening, a blink—then the air starts up. When it cannot finish, when it lifts but does not land, it hangs. On the Isle of Grief the air drapes on us and we do not part it and we do not leave. Shoulders, lids and arms droop like curtains.

We call our time a day. The sun and moon sit opposite, circles of time and no time. We stay all that day and the next, as possible as birds, our hands opening and closing on captive air

Lynn Strongin
Victoria, British Columbia
Summer 2010

Acknowledgements

Thanks to the following journals who first published, in one form or another, some of the included pieces:

3rd Bed
Caketrain
elimae
Upstairs at Duroc
Whalelane

For Barbara and Don

The Statuary Garden

The up cutting of the curve is sometimes all the distinction
between the mouldings of far-distant countries
and utterly strange nations.

John Ruskin,
on the Gothic dripstone

A particular anger helped move the ground I worked in, the soil in which bulbs would be buried inches down—some of them dropped hastily because the digger is cold; forced to right themselves against all they would ever know of the earth, then sit in numbing frigid vaults for long and longer months trying to believe themselves safe in the dirt, though I had left it uneven, easy to dig into, attractively obvious to squirrels and birds. Well, what else could I do, the landscaper—the bulbs themselves—did not say to do anything else.

My first stab into the ground found a lone bulb already in place. I don't know where it came from.

After I could take no more, I washed my hands (diligent about the nails) and changed my muddied yard pants for something cleaner, softer, corduroy, and not long later found myself walking by a bookstore on 2nd Avenue where, on a five-shelf case in the corner of the window, I saw a copy of *My Life* by Isadora Duncan. I went in and picked it up. It was green, embossed and clearly well cared for. Inside, someone had pressed a large leaf against the cover—maybe madrona, but pretty wide for madrona, maybe rubber tree. No handwritten name or stamp offered clues to where it had come from or what it had meant to anyone.

But mostly I had been tired all day and, when not on my knees in the garden or staring at rows of books—in other words, when I was walking—I had to sit numerous times wherever I could and that is what I did with that book, my back bent a little forward, elbows on knees, thoughts in close, hands close too, but also as far from me as they have ever been.

After such another rest, I bought the book, and as I was leaving the store I noticed a display of old magazines near the Café, a coffee corner I had avoided—so noisy, so spilled-onto, so terrible to look at, chaos remarkable when everything surrounding it was cased or in alphabetical order. I don't know what kind of people would want to go there.

I skirted the wall, taking with me a magazine with an advertisement for Steinway pianos, a piece Rockwell Kent had illustrated with an angel—heroic, of course—flying against night and sea, suspended by thousands of engraved lines, free as a chord in a white kind of diving shape with hands turned up slightly, ready to part the water but easy against the air, not diving but going through. The knees were bent so its delicate white feet would clear the mountains and the hats of those in the street (who might not, anyway, notice an angel's touch), but not so bent that the toes would not pleasantly graze the soft tops of hemlocks and yews, the way pendant fingers make lazy chevrons as they dangle from a boat.

I carried the magazine under an arm that claimed to still feel such things. My feet trailed over nothing but the way home and, once inside, I put the magazine on a table—certain no angel would want a chair but might agree to lie in profile on a round, small, wooden surface happy to have a being on it shaped in a kind of *S*.

I meant to write more about something else but was

distracted by the De Chirico print, *L'Angoisse du depart*—a thing so confident of itself it could have chosen to hang anywhere. I don't know why it feels like that or why it would select this place and why looking at it, though it was thrilling, also made me think about the bulbs and what I had done to them. Asleep, dead, alive . . . . Who was I to say they must be everything?

In just a few days I had enacted one violence after another, now planting, now wringing tea from bags I had scalded and exposed to light. I'd left a trail of the anguished, only some of them intact.

De Chirico did not paint the box in the foreground of the picture, he painted the shadow on it, the impending absence, an explanatory puff in the distance, a voice for which there is no voice for.

As for the Dresdner monkey, the porcelain violinist in the Harry Lane print next over on the wall—the tailed musician flanked by roses—maybe Harry painted that, maybe he didn't, but he did not paint the variety of petals, their green reflective vase or the drape, seductive as silk, falling against the table. I don't know how all those things even got there. It was not my fault; nor mine the perturbations of white light.

It had been a difficult day, framed by the discovery of additional work which I had hoped would be new but was instead simply pending, when the whole point became that I had lost my pen—an easy thing to lose, a pen, of little significance (it was not a Waterbrook), but suddenly it became the need behind everything.

I knelt to descend into that unseen area below my desk, a place, as under a small shrub, that normally does not need my thinking about it, and began to fumble around in the dark. The longer my hand was out of sight, away and moving further and further from me, the more vulnerable I felt—stuck out there in possibility; I mean, who knows?

My hand became a thing of its own, going resolvedly forward (though what it understood of true search I don't know), and in a kind of alarm I bent myself a bit more and leaned in so I could get a good look at it again. As I did so, in the briefest of moments, I thought I saw another hand approaching from the opposite direction, feeling toward mine as if to seek it out.

Well, I do not believe in mirrors, and the evening was getting on and on so I stood up and let the whole matter go.

~

Outside, one April holiday, with some indefinite thing on my mind, I headed to a spot of the yard I seldom visit. Here I thought to relax a little, no one suggesting that I affirm or reject anything, or hunt for eggs in a festive way, no more than would Captain Roggeveen in 1722, as he considered the withered grass, the scorched rocks, the lack of trees, suggest it of the Easter Islanders (on my mind this day.)

A kind of *rongo rongo* chant stayed with me as I padded across the lawn: a chant of Moai and windy knolls, of need that turns the future to a ghost and places one statue to look inland, all others seaward to face head-on the tsunamis and, worse than that, the rescue. I walked cautiously toward the corner that borders the yard with the big dog.

The high wood fence kept the wind off me, the sun out of my eyes, and the pit bull at safe distance while I surveyed the beds. Nevertheless, he charged—black but for the flecked mouth, the red sockets. I tossed him something store-bought, a biscuit, a cheap prayer, and whispered his name urgently: "*Gotto, Gotto, hey Gotto, good boy.*" I don't know who'd want to keep such a dog.

This framed corner of the yard is as far as safety goes, as far in its way as an island is from any place else in the Pacific; an extreme windward position.

I planned to plant something near the lucifers, to take out the rhododendron, erect a trellis, pergola, gazebo—and now thought about it quickly, staking out change as the beast slathered over his treat; as he forgot for a while to run at the fence and slam against it, to barrel into it again and again, to bend and crack it until finally bursting through, tearing his face, his back and feet with splinters and nails and causing God knows what.

I wanted something else (I always wanted something else) and thought the black-edged sinew that circled the koi pond and held in the water might contain it. In the center (it was a large pond) I noticed an island the shape of Pohnpei. Micronesia was there whenever it was wanted, though I was not precisely sure how it had gotten there—its arrangements of flowing, close leaves, its rocks and ferns and elevations . . . I would have known it anywhere.

A heron dangled its long legs over the water, dipping, not feeling. The island, the pond, responded in kind—involving, not inviting. Such things require us to look, and so I always do in my natural way of greeting. In return, the island floats and dazzles, rains within itself and makes a sky. I have never wanted to travel, but my heart rolls each time I see it.

Desire is the most unaccommodating sense. I often speak about the pond in small texts, how snails sweep it clean every day, but I do not often speak about the island.

One day, under water, all the pond animals died all at once. Why I don't know. Their skeletons and shells settled close together around the island as a reef.

One night, I left the heat down too low overnight and woke up shuddering. In the shower, to warm up, I turned the water up too high and burned my shoulder. The spot, what I could see of it, looked like Corsica.

Looking out the window, I saw robins tearing worms from the ground everywhere I had disturbed it.

~

She was there in the shade garden of the north side when I moved in: the simple "Sophia," a statue and circulating fountain, prominent among cypress shrubs and ferns, placed around the corner where it was invisible from the deck, the koi pond, the lindens, the round herb garden.

Sophia's head-mounted vessel tipped relentlessly, spilling water down her front and back, baptizing her to the point of whatever death is eventually available to her. Watching for just a while made me tired and I wanted to sit down. There were no inscriptions other than her name, so I could not tell who made her—she who splashed elegance so casually, as if it did not cost. As circular as yearning, as ghosts that cannot kiss; beauty poured to pour again . . . . What good could come of this? She looked at me deliberately, like the moon.

The rest of the garden was sparse, not overgrown and woven as I have seen gardens and jungles to be, not anything for Rousseau—no red sun, no jaguar on the man or on the man's shadow (whichever it is that flees); yet something dies in it just the same, year after year.

The landscaper's crew did the heavy lifting, dragging two recumbent white stone animals from the back of the truck: sphinxes, more leonine than Egyptian, more Sumerian, but disinclined to fly. They were wrestled, hefted and carted to the deck amid shouts of "Sinew, boys, sinew!" "Leverage! Traction and muscle, boys, traction and muscle!" The landscaper gained from his detachment an almost levitating strength. He directed the objects into place at the top of the steps where they would funnel the eye down toward the plants lining the walk, the pots of exploding purple grass, the pergola furthest away. Then everyone stepped back to look. And there they sat, looking back at us. *Sinew,* I always think when I descend between them.

More statues were brought in and later I had to move one, had to shift it just slightly for balance. I tried not to damage the worms that must be busy beneath it pushing away the earth and eating, closing the burrows they open each night, recovering from being pressed upon all day—these poor crawlers who provide in smallness a kind of hope for the world that I, by balancing, try to increase.

I was horrified, though not surprised, to see holes made all over the beds by squirrels who'd hauled out many of the bulbs I'd planted and exposed the poor worms, their fellow territorials (though to be fair worms are, in a sense, semi-aquatic and squirrels are not.)

According to Darwin's study of them, earthworms have been found at heights of 1,500 feet in Scotland; yet, on a heath in Surrey, only a few castings could be detected on paths very much inclined at all. I don't know if Darwin discusses it, but sometimes breathing is hard, on ground as under water, and at any time anything can be futile. If he did say something about any of this, I don't know where to find it.

Sometimes, walking back to the house, halfway up the steps to the deck, I pause and hear the ground make its smallest movements.

~

A fellow came to paint the wood for the arbor going up over the concrete slab just outside the family room slider, that and a small bench. He did a great job and I thanked him, paid him and admired his work, though I felt, I don't know why, I was in another place altogether.

~

I wanted to buy a calendar, but instead when I went out I bought an urn, a lavish, large pot with angelic creatures clinging to the top. Its rust and supporting square base bore portions of a vision of Versailles. I have no idea what perfection is or if it is affected by a deep rent down one of the angel's backs, a gap as sharp as the Mid-Atlantic Rift when it rises in Iceland. This gash had claimed one wing. The two contemplatives stood on lion's heads and gripped the rim as they stared steadily and deeply into emptiness.

It is a habit of man and nature to adapt to each other. I thought I might sit on the new bench and consider how these sprites manage, but began to worry that if I looked too long they might sense it and look up. So I got up and went inside.

~

Beyond my fence with its sturdy, close fitting boards, I believe there are trees in fine, rich soil covering old lava sheets and, among the trees, luxuriant bunch grass.

Inside, the garden has a continental clime. Far from maritime influences it is a small region of mild relief, ringed by large classical forms: orators, maidens, swans and mythical beasts. Beside a lilac is a carved sphere with four equidistant bees. I have identified my garden's temperate zones: soil, loess, plains, hillocks; crests, ridges, ranges, peaks—which, though I know nothing of fractals, repeat the world in nature as, by lettering, the images by draftsmen bring objects into being.

In the mail, a packet of postcards: La Porte Saint-Denis,

the Pyramid of Cestius, Teatro Anatomico of Padua.

~

The workers were finished and long gone when I noticed from the dining room window, which faces straight toward the pergola (though my eyes now stop at the urn), that someone had placed the small stone pelican between the arms of a sphinx. I had lost track of it and now it had become a detail from Merson's *Rest on the Flight into Egypt,* a painting in which some of the Holy Family sleeps, apparently in the arms of the Sphinx, but mostly in a strange light. Someone did not want the bird to get lost. The darker pages of scripture are one thing, haven and wing another, so I resisted going outside even to look and left everything as it was.

~

As instructed, I sprinkled bulb food on the ground and plant food on the new plants, watering it in and smoothing the bark with the back of a loose rake.

Often, when gardening, I think of other places, of Shorey's, the Roosevelt Café or even Magnolia Hi-Fi where motivated young staff in suits show me the high-end equipment that makes sound larger and finer, that gives to pictures a sharpness that seems to come from an altogether new way of seeing. Sometimes I just have to sit and let everything come at me from all sides.

It is tiring to tire so easily and I already had, that morning, as I approached the strip mall. So, I was not particularly aware of my surroundings (though I have been warned to be) when two kids on skateboards roared up from behind me like twin trains and set me spinning by a shoulder.

Well, I was raised to keep myself to the inside when walking, the outside when riding, and was unprepared for sound or blow. I shouted after them, compiling pain from its furthest reaches and pumping it into a fist, a coiled peony wilting toward the walk.

I believe in expectation and embarrassment so did not look around but got up in a wooden way and leaned against a post. My hands, as they steadied me, sensed that the diameter of the post grew narrower the higher it stood from the ground. Planted much deeper than the four inches marked on my trowel, it had no need for discomfort or struggle, needn't bloom or please me in any way. I was humbled. *"Bless the bulbs, the grass, the trees and all spiring things in the name of this post,"* I thought. I heard the words as if they were in the air and for a moment did not know where I was.

~

Sunday, the traditional morning of regret, I woke in worry in the dark, my imagination awash with images of animals scrabbling, twigs cracking and beaks tearing the tenders that hold things up; of fish tossed out and strangling on a stone. Anything can happen in a place that shows its scars to you.

I am no *naïf*, I know that things disappear, vessels

break, fingerprints go unidentified. Machines do, the earth does, and dogs do doggedly the most unimaginable things. An unrelenting stratum of trouble rises and does its ruptive best—though I like to presume that my familiars in it wait for me, unmolested, by the steps. I feared for them.

I shook myself in alarm, threw on my clothes, snapped back the shades, turned on the lights, washed the dishes, vacuumed the carpets, straightened the pictures and adjusted the chairs into smaller and smaller conversation groups. Then I buckled up my high mud boots, put on my woolly coat with the two rows of buttons, my aviator's hat with the down earflaps and strode across the room. I opened wide the paneled door to the backyard. My eyes took in everything, and threatened to keep looking.

~

"No, no, no," the landscaper said. "The snow drops, the fritillaria go right into the lawn, not the beds . . . for naturalizing."

I slipped off my garden shoes. Obviously I would have to think about things in a different way. I made coffee, slipped Sibelius into the CD player and settled into a soft chair where the long rays of the sun could warm my shoulders through the window. No use, I thought, trying to find them and dig them up. I would have to get more bulbs.

I don't know how I got to be so lucky. I can walk to most places from my home though it requires crossing in traffic to do so. As cars around here do not normally slow even for their own kind, attention is called for, as is bright clothing and, if possible, height. I am lucky to be so tall.

I stopped at a bus kiosk to rest and managed to hum five or six parts of the *Goldberg Variations* before feeling I'd better move on, in case a bus should approach and see me and misinterpret everything.

The building next on my right going north was the co-op where prescription renewals awaited me for anti-allergens and acid blockers. I approached the two, big, out-swinging doors, anticipating the visual happiness of the rock wall sculpture inside, water running down it like a falls, and the Italian villa prints with lavenders, olives and pines. As I reached out, the door suddenly swung open from within, but I pulled back quickly and saved my fingers. Luck was everywhere with me that day.

Further along the street, I noticed that the hardware store had a special sale on LED string icicles. Two would do for my new arbor. Lately, evening had been coming on too early, disappointing me when I still wanted light. I went in, switching in my mind from Glenn Gould to the orchestral version of the *Variations,* the populist arrangement despised by the *cognoscenti.*

At the Deli, as the clerk made a sandwich for me, I saw a washcloth come very close to touching a slice of bread. After the clerk served me and walked away, I peeled off the crust, though this exposed everything and made containment less certain. At that point I'd spent all the money I had on me so I went home to bury myself in a book. A car honked as I cleared the road.

~

I believe that, in their hearts, even the smallest animals sense what they are.

My feet cramp. I seldom go out. Each sunny day hurts my eyes. My fingers tighten in the cold and turn white. At night my heart weighs itself against its better deeds and is not lightened, and often I have appointments so plain I cannot even think what they are for.

~

Clearly, a change was called for. Easter was one thing, Christmas another.

When the train finally stopped at the holiday shopping town in the mountains, I stood to look out through my visible breath into an American *Weihnachtmarkt* where—left and right—lights, tinsel and shopping stalls waited.

As I was handed down by the porter, I noticed a smudge of coal on my glove and shuddered. I thought: here was so much Bavaria where it should not be, and here am I and it is not going to be warm—but didn't think the rest of that thought, not until later when I had tired from walking (I always tire from walking), from looking and hoping, primarily hoping for a new coat. Then I began to worry that I might never be warm again, there or any other place. How preposterous it was to go on and on as if a coat could make a difference or a glove when there were people everywhere around me, closing in on me, people and limbs, jostling, hanging, limbs of trees, trees of people without coats, flying limbs, limbs stuck in the snow, trains full of people without coats or shoes, dead limbed and unlimbed people and the not-yet-dead who had nothing in them anymore that would strive to warm them—limbs, limbs, limbs and people like refugees stacked along the railway . . . . I had to take a deep, cold breath.

I don't know where horror comes from. It must be planted down deep. Earlier, when that whistle blew, that awful piercing shriek as I stepped off the train, my mind was pulled away though I tried hard to hold on. And now, after shopping (this was why I'd come after all), I don't know, I just felt so lonely—the cold of the walkway climbing steadily up toward the heart—and then I began to fear that the train would not come back for me.

Near to me was the King Ludwig Bier Stube. Taking the steps down into the beer garden, I found a warm and noisy room with long tables crowded with merrymakers and beer in tall glasses, all surrounded by puddles of wine and suds. Sweat ran down the windows and down a multitude of waitresses, perfect wet waitresses with rosy faces and huge slippery breasts that nevertheless helped them hold up and carry enormous trays of sweating mugs—cold to the cold—as they serpentined through the noise, the rows of rotisseried birds behind them . . . . I took my old coat off. An accordion player with lederhosen and thick wool socks rolled up to his knees (socks with a flower on them, I don't know which flower but socks with a flower on them) squeezed music into the din and a woman played a kind of zither and someone did the chicken dance—hardly an organized dance at all, a humiliating jumble in the middle of the floor of flapping and bobbing, of strutting and scratching as if in the dirt, hands angled high under the arms.

Everyone laughed at this winged person and I began to feel—I am ashamed to say this, I can't even think if this is the real word for this—*safe* in that messy room with transformative arms and the accordion pumping out the guiltiest of pleasures and even worse than that, I felt a kind of jealousy, maybe the reverse of jealousy, I don't know, a jealous confidence that I was part of this already and always had been and many, many others were not; that I among few was included in this exclusive band.

Inclusive, exclusive, that's when the vision of the limbs came in again for an awful moment, my own and those of everyone, except the chicken man who had given some of his away.

Clips, letters, money, pens (or what sounded like these things) clattered to the floor, shaken underfoot from pockets, and in all of this, the man's ridiculous pair of shoes supported a cargo of short, striped socks, bulging calves and stomach and a small, green hat. It became a kind of wallpaper: the beer, the faces, the sweat, the heat we were making—breathing not dancing—and for an instant I believed yes, I was safe in this charming, festive danger.

But, as I sat and watched longer into the afternoon, the crowd calling again for the same silly song, the room drifted away from me, though still as open as a stage. I felt cold again, apprehensive—should a massive hand reach in to rearrange us; should everyone, as soon as touched, freeze suddenly in place and then, maybe, rise into the air.

By the time I was due back at the train my feet had swelled beyond recognition. It was hard for me to get up. My hands were beet red. I could not even tell they were mine.

Snow had fallen intermittently on my trip into and back from the mountains and steadily, heavily at home; the reverse of what I'd expected. I believe in the present, that the shadows of clouds on the ground are as high and wide as the real things above—not the theory of the shaken globe, exactly, but like canvases with the backgrounds already carefully painted in—so disproportion startles me.

Caroming through a channel of drifts and berms, I stopped at what looked like the front of my driveway. There was no pulling in. White covered every surface. The pavement was indistinguishable from the lawn and all of it was higher. Snow had climbed the flowering pear and golden chain and now peered at me from atop the branches, wondering who I was. The car would have to sit where it was in the road.

Staying in the center of the porch, away from the lengthening bolts of icicles on the eaves, I struggled up the steps, lifting my cold knees high like slow, old pumps. Inside, things were as they had been. I changed into fleece and made tea, then I opened the blinds to the nearly invisible backyard. Snow covered the urn and the bees and piled high against the fence. Only the ears of the sphinxes could be seen. I saw no animal prints, nor could I see around the corner to the meditation garden where

Sophia, dulled down when the pipes were closed off, idly piled on white disguise.

I stood for a long while, feeling as if I were partly inside and partly out, as if I were in the sort of William M. Thompson print from the 1940's: a snowy forest, stream, a cabin under the trees with glowing windows and smoke trailing across the white roof as if to write a message. I had no idea who might be inside such a cabin. But here I was, looking in, while everything outside the cabin and my own house lay frozen and white except for the under-branchings of trees and a path of moving water squeezed by iced-up banks.

Sometimes, in those prints, there are sunrises — large and orange. My own would be delayed by several more hours. I pulled the blinds to preserve heat, turned on all the downstairs lights, lit the fire, put on the Arrau recording of Chopin's *Nocturnes and Interludes* and sat down.

~

If I could give you a few minutes, as you are floating up the canal just now, the kind of feeling I had when I had done my work.

John Ruskin,
"Stones of Venice"

Lost Secrets of Meteorology

I am going back a little, but the strangeness remains, as if I had an inner glow.

Cees Nooteboom,
"The Following Story"

Snow began on Tower Mountain November 18 and has not, by this ninetieth day of entombment, stopped. The hours Ed spends watching movies are uncountable to the point where in his dreams it is the great white whale himself climbing the mast to be shot by young Jim Hawkins and the once-marooned Hands who beckon the whalers out to sea.

This week there is a ship in everything he chooses, though sea must change and so will he, to a savannah, a jungle, a WWII chicken coop with Richard Burton. He must ultimately wash the dishes and straighten up the house— but after *Captain Blood,* after *Bluebeard,* after *Titanic.*

Mostly, he knows already what he sees, cueing the dialog and plot, weeding through documentaries, specials and the custodial dead zone of late-night programming.

When he prepares for sleep but cannot reach it, a scene may come back to him, something not quite clear or sensible or the germ of something else he would like to see on screen one day. When that happens, he writes notes to himself or flushes something out to resolution, peace of mind so tied to a good ending. He may write for hours.

He welcomes night and its thoughts. Cut off, in fortress, he wants to record everything, to let nothing leave him—not celluloid, digital or the imaginary—and since the details of cinema are already what they are, it is mostly the invented he sets down.

Outside, behind a flurry, over the clouds, above the wind, the sun rises and sets and each day drifts some measure to the south, a burdened, leaning tree. He changes frequently to the Weather Channel, reciting with the meteorologist the norms, expressing surprise at the lows, comparing snowfall by volume to rain per square inch—to return, like a furloughed commander, a director, an editor, like God himself, to the middle of narrative.

In truth, he has inclined to a life of observation since the days of the test pattern, has always immersed himself in the medium that does not tan or wet. A human isobar, he is harmonious, co-existent, the equal of those around him, but as shown clearly enough on the screen, destined not to cross or touch another.

Seasons unwind and coil, push and pull. He has set the inside temperature at sixty-eight, augments it with fire, restores it by window. Forced this year by eight plus feet of snow to maintain even more intensely a life he has always preferred, he is nonetheless neither blind nor indifferent. He has seen the unpredictable rhythms of his own life ebb and flow, and so to the extent he can, he will control it by remote.

Note to the programmers:

Is it irony or cruelty itself to present mid-winter a program of sun-drenched, Italian songs and Andrea Bocelli? There he is, comfortable, shirt open, reflecting joy and desert heat. We sense his pleasure; we fall in love with it, the anticipated pleasure of caress, but after awhile our feral selves—that watch from the trees, that answer the song with howls, that rend meat in the downed fences—that part of us longs to complete the circuit.

And so, on this frozen bathtub of a night, we are plunged into the desire of a whole countryside. It is harmless enough, it is imagination, it is television.

But, another part of us wants always to be true; and so our skins lift slightly, expectantly, pathetically, for the sun's sweet touch. How we miss it and how we fail, no options open for us this time of night but arena football and the evangelicals.

A proposed scene:

She stands with her back to them. What is she doing? Does she need to be doing something? In their minds she does. They watch her back, inanimate at first, then a little active at the shoulders and the neck as her head cocks.

They've finished with lunch, and while they are still talking, she's stood up without a word and walked away—not far, but away. Their talk trails off and the two men look at each other and then at her back.

"Victoria?" one of them says to her.

"Yes..."

"Are you OK?"

"Of course."

"What are you doing?"

"Nothing," she replies. "Go on with your conversation."

That is difficult in that what they want to talk about just now is Victoria, who only has her back to them and can certainly hear.

One of them says, "Um, well . . . ."

The other interrupts, "Great sandwiches!"

"It's true," she says after a pause, as if her voice were coming

from the future, "I didn't realize. Who would think?"

"What?" one of the men asks.

"Well," she goes on in place, "something occurred to me while you were eating and talking. Some feeling . . . . I'd almost forgotten . . . Something . . . . Well, anyway, it made me think and I had to get up and see."

"Yes?"

"I don't mean anything by it, don't be offended, it's just that . . . OK, it's just that you both seem so much more real to me when I can't see you. I'd almost forgotten how it was . . . I mean, back then . . . . This beautiful cabinet, this golden light in the middle, the voices who could be anyone from anywhere in the world who could say just anything.

"Oh God, I miss radio so much."

~

It is not an empty life Ed lives, nor the static, derived life of reality shows. No, events both real and unreal touch him. One afternoon he learned of The Great Flood of 1993, and though it happened in a place he does not know, he feels it keenly.

It started with the wettest June on record in the Midwest and was expected to lead to the usual dry summer, but not so. A series of storm systems lingered and lingered some more. Persistent downpours ran off into the upper Mississippi and its tributaries. Rivers rose to record levels. Levees collapsed (he aches for the levees.) The Mississippi crested at 49.4 feet at St. Louis (he aches for St. Louis.) By the end of July, 16,000 square miles were under water—an area roughly the size of Massachusetts, Connecticut, and Rhode Island combined (he aches for the out of breath)—the missing and dead all over the place, the living scattered, grass widows of the vast, drowned plains.

It snows another eight inches on Ed's house, big white fluffs innocent of their own volume. His uncle's carport collapses from avalanche when the dog balks at the outside and the uncle slams the door.

His cat complains loudly about the litter box. Ed surveys his home mournfully, his own soiled nest. He can hear that the neighbors two houses away are listening to Handel's *Messiah* though Christmas is well past. As the piece progresses and their redemptive joys abound, the volume rises to levels that maim his ability to think.

It is a day of excess that Ed addresses with awe or chill as circumstances suggest.

Note re: The Messiah

Handel is blameless for the behavior of sheep and for the Full Rhyme scheme this passage nicely demonstrates:

All we like sheep have gone astray,
everyone in his own way.

Herd animals stray from the shearer and the shorn. Sheep slip under a fence not sheep tight, and some say that as one goes, so go they all. It is a divine mercy that each knows the voice of its shepherd, one from another, though flocks be many and many voices raised up.

Handel celebrates the supposed dismay over those who wander off while quixotically believing in Heaven's greater exaltation when a single lost lamb, etc. But as the joy of recovery necessarily fades to examination, is the ultimate chill among the hosts as savored by the lamb as the solitary chill of the rocks? We want to die in nature, where we live.

As for actually counting them—lost, found, food or eyeing a sharp ridge—with the irregular plural, sheep means one and many at the same time.

Not sheep nor sleep be mine this night; nor shepherd nor the tangling path of the labyrinth.

Proposed documentary on geometry, wool and water:

An error in the calculation of the span of apples and the concentricities of trees, or tracks of crows beside the lark. The serrate margins of a dress caress the parquetry and draw the heart as upward from a choked well.

Transforming lines and fault extend the hands. Oily wool grows tighter than its brother—a kingdom lost—and yet we find the raisins in an ambered bee.

The problem lies in stepping-swimming over. The garroted fruit ascends its God and, on occasion, a bulb will rather die than show you anything. You obliterate with chalk the fossil relatives of time, but mind the subsets. The calendars of skin follow on the fence. We come from brew, a property that wants to live in water since it can, but we angle from a boat—our X, the small red bob on string, floating outward from the mean.

Light lets itself out, then out again and out. What it tires of standing for is gone from where it touched. A door slams, a traveling punch. The good armies of darkness trample what you mourn and welcome; inhaling what you cannot leave, which is the air.

Something says goodnight to something it forgets.

~

Ed was born in 1947, in Seattle, within eyeshot of Mt. Rainier, the same month that UFOs were famously seen to hover over the dormant volcano and Mt. Tahoma, its smaller side peak. This signal event and his royal names, Edward George, seduced him to assume a special status. Anything might be possible, earth to sky. He could be a visitor, a very important one. He could go mad. He could abdicate. Or lift off.

One night, in the violent evening storms that call a halt to summer, the heavens heaved, lightning sliced through the trees, and wind whirled down on the house like a funnel. Thunder pounded the mountain again and again as if to flatten it.

As he watched from inside, the whole roof above him seemed to peel away. He felt an electricity worthy of him. He gaped and stared straight up and then, as if he were inside a flare, he suddenly saw everything. Everything! His mind was unable to frame such radiance, but he took it in, the whole of it, clearly and truly, inside and out of time.

What he saw entered his eyes and kept on going through tubes and wash. Its whiteness coursed through his red. It made large of the small and small of the large as it coursed and covered and lifted, a wave over and under what is never the same as it was.

On its way past memory it slowed and slipped into his heart, adding beats to those Ed had always thought to be enough.

Sometimes he assumes the lotus position in the center of his bed, present and not present, anointed, alert to the wandering attentions of his cat, the shifting reflections of headlights on photos, the intricate winds of his inner chambers.

Other times he agrees to sit open and calm before the television and review the parade before him, each of a kind, each of a quality. He makes his judgments.

Notes for a series:

One day a little family began. It did not start out intending to be small. It formed in the usual way and then, because it was attractive, gathered others to it. As the nucleus was not large or forceful, however, it did not retain them very well. Spouses, friends and small children flew out from time to time as from a giant crack-the-whip, their faces lit with surprise and momentary thrill.

Charted over time, the energy of this group remained a constant. Truth be told, the family was not unhappy this way. It prized itself as itself.

And little wonder. Its members captured attention like an approach of weather. Among and between them were musicians, surgeons, artists and aviators; charismatics; wealthy, quixotic, generous and explosive romantics; scholars, hermits, woodworkers, contemplatives, seers, effetes. Each flared in one or more or all of its interesting ways, amazing others, entertaining themselves, an aurora borealis of a family.

Within an aurora, streamers or arches of light appear, caused by the emission of light from atoms excited by electrons accelerated along magnetic lines. Similarly, families emit excitement, each according to its lights.

One day, out of the blue, forces of containment, perhaps in the stratosphere where weather changes but little, began to take aim at this little family on earth and pick off its members, one by one.

The casual observer might not note the steadily lessening size and influence of this already tiny group, but within it the absences were mounting like holes in the ozone.

The current hole in the ozone is now a little bigger than Antarctica.

The same observer would see the path of this family as smooth. It appeared to age normally in all its levels; it got on. At close-up, its progress was as rutted as washboards, as strained as cleats.

Nevertheless, in trouble or at peace, it sensed its distinctions, valued its similarities and held together whether in potato cellars or lecture circuits; an armada of a family, running seaward and generally clear of the rocks.

Armadas are made up of warships, fishing vessels or other moving gatherings we can see, such as a belt of meteorites, or other things we do not see very well. From space our atmosphere appears as a thin, blue veil sailing around the world.

The rate of meteor activity in the atmosphere is greatest near dawn when the earth's orbital motion is in the direction of the dawn terminator. Earth scoops up meteoroids on the dawn side of the planet and outruns them on the dusk side, reminiscent of the behaviors of a following tide or youngest child.

There is evidence in early rock formations of an anaerobic reducing atmosphere containing the elements in their reduced states.

The polar winter leads to the formation in the stratosphere of a vortex drawing air from the upper layers of the atmosphere and lower mesosphere.

Stratospheric clouds comprise the home of lesser gods who, when sunlight returns to the polar regions of the hemispheres, are again able to see faint details of the earth through holes in the ozone, the vacancies caused by chlorine and bromine compounds in catalytic destruction cycles. The gods are mildly distracted by what they see and enhance their lazy joys by gaming. The object of one such game is to reach for what they can barely see below and remove the greatest number of them. Isolates and small groups, especially if they shine, are targets of convenience.

These removals are called Chapman Reactions after S. Chapman in "A Theory of Upper-Atmosphere Ozone", Mem. Roy. Meteorol. Soc., 1930. Such reactions include a sensation in mortals not unlike the sudden onset of winter.

Such a sensation may be like a veil, of which there are many kinds: lengths of protective or ornamental netting for the head or face; any of various liturgical cloths, especially to cover a chalice; material which hides, obscures, disguises or softens tonal distortion; interventions through which it is difficult to see; sheer things; membranes or other covering body parts; things to be lifted or assumed by a nun.

Of all the veils, the thin blue one, in particular, is the most exquisite and magical.

~

If he is not careful this day, he will watch *The Godfather* once again, for a time beyond too many. It is that or *The Simian Line,* a Lynn Redgrave/Harry Connick/William Hurt movie from 2001, with a sound track and color quality of two decades prior. He checks the Weather Channel.

"Notice how we can locate high and low pressure zones by these lines on the maps," the young meteorologist intones. "Also," he reminds, looking straight at Ed, "remember that winds flow from high to low areas. This allows us to predict local patterns."

Nothing new to be learned here, so he wanders back to the movie. There are ghosts in it, unseen except by children and a palm reader. The ghosts are not greatly unhappy. You can tell which characters portray them since the theme "*The River is Wide*" plays when one appears.

The outdoor scenes were shot on the river between Manhattan and New Jersey. In one view the moon stands right above the river, in another it is elsewhere, then suddenly we are shown a moonless street and the tiny leaves of a locust. Reflections, boats, relationships, time, everything is flowing; the sun, too. A ghost says, "Things are changing all the time."

Nothing new from ghosts either, so Ed considers the simian line, the transverse palmar crease, when the so-called heart lines and head lines are not separate but cross the palm as one. The trait is common in nonhuman primates, but because this movie is only a little about the past, nothing devolves. The simian line, which has all manner of medical, superstitious and pejorative associations, is discussed only as predictive tool.

It is a day of surfaces, repetition and parallels that Ed does not resist. He fits the remote firmly in his right hand, pressing it against his palm, pointing it and turning up the volume. He will stay with this movie that is, in its own way, earnest.

Were the TV meteorologist also a radiologist tuned in to *The Simian Line,* he might turn companionably toward the audience and suggest taking radiographs of the hand and finger bones to locate high and low pressure zones correspondent to lines and ridges and then show how the skin of the hand flows from high to low areas allowing us to identify individual patterns.

Ed prefers *The Godfather,* its formality and romance, its dependable cartoon warriors, the creepy exchangeable violence and a belief in itself so great that it transports—but it goes on to eleven o'clock. He will abide and hope there is something worthwhile at eight.

In the meantime, the ghosts are appealing—Hurt, a Civil War gentleman; Samantha Mathis, a Roaring Twenties party girl—though Ed is greatly disappointed not to have seen so far a single monkey.

Notes for a short film about ghosts:

"This is the short tale of the life of the valiant knight and patriot Aleksey Alekseevich Alekseev," she reads. She has jumped to an end that sounds like a beginning but is not in a hurry, just having trouble getting through. Smoke drifting over the page hides the words she wants to read. It does not just obscure them—that is, the words, wherever the smoke goes, seem to be missing altogether. Clouds blow over her eyes, words come back and others leave. It gives her the fizzy feel of neon. Flash on, flash off, ptzzzzzzz, etc. She reads Daniil Kharms in disconnect:

"Then he Polish fashion, holds out....
his hat, and say, "Give Jesus." That helped.
Aleksy Aleksee ....
without food."
Ptzzzzzzz. . . .

Her husband, the collector, is away; in his office or a shop; elsewhere. And as collectors prize the copy closest to the source—an uncorrected book proof, the author's marginalia—so her husband dreams of her younger self, trying to keep her just the same while her mother, foraging through decades of damaged memory to identify her, finds and names an imagined, if oddly familiar girl, Little Susan. "Where is Little Susan? She was just here, I saw her. Where is my Little Susan?"

Big Susan hears a sound like ptzzzzzzz, then a thwack as her book falls to the floor. The words are clear now but closed to her. She reaches to put out a cigarette and rubs her finger and thumb together to remove ash in the way one suggests something costly. She would not say 'marginalia' around the husband who lusts for an easier past nor would she look for Little Susan in herself or for the missing daughter of a mother living backwards.

She goes to the archway beyond which her young Fred practices the piano as he does daily, shaded by the street-side lindens. He is otherworldly in constancy, but an indifferent talent. Finished, he lowers the harp-shaped lid onto the body, pressing firm hands on the bright polish and tries not to think of his mother, who is dead.

Susan believes she is moving and speaking to her son, but it is only a plan of mind. Her eyes skirt the room as on covered feet and suddenly she is thinking of her husband, the investment banker and rare book dealer, a man of speculation. She remembers a delicate privacy between them. Turning to hide her blush, she thinks again in the general direction of her son: "Goodnight, Fred." He trudges in his lonely way to his room. She stands at the window and looks toward Frankfurt.

It is a strain to look directly, to remember. A vision intrudes of her uncle at a window in Sonora, anticipating the arrival of prisoners. He smirks to think of their broad backs, corded wrists, their ankles flayed by chains. He, too, is a kind of banker. As she turns from thinking of him, his heart pools as if he has never existed, but birds, terrified to think he exists everywhere, sing as they have never sung before. Everything seems to happen at once.

Her husband leaves his office on Mainzer Allee with a

package. "This would have amused her," he thinks. He stops for tobacco, thoughts wisping away in the fog.

"He will be here soon," she thinks. "Werner, my husband." Pipe smoke trails him to the door then tumbles over him to slip in ahead. In the room are traces of dust, a book, the muddled hum of Fredrick—cameo of a son—all evoking her absence.

He grasps the doorknob with a deep breath and pushes forcefully as if to say: "To the barricades!" When he removes his hat, he sees that he has scraped his shoes. His composure is lost.

"Werner!" she thinks with delight as the door opens. She senses the movement of his feet on the carpet and has trouble with the rhythm: right .... left ... ri ... . She fears he will stumble. She drops something, there is a flicker, a flash, and her mind slips off to other moments. She sees him, earlier, on the hill in his car; behind him, the street by the bank; before that, his desk where he sits dreaming. "He comes home to me," she thinks happily. "But maybe he will scuff his shoes. He will bend to wipe them with a cloth and something will hit him. A streetcar, a train. We will never be together."

He enters the bedroom. She turns with the speed of an engine, sensing the straight of the tracks, the surprisingly dull wheels, the lurch of the steering bar.

"I will never have mourned her enough," he sighs.

He changes his shoes and, when he stands, tightens his shoulders as though to keep something from falling off.

Notes on motivation:

We couldn't leave the Isle of Grief as there is no conveyance.

Had there been one, we surely would have left on it.

Water, rocks and trees are there, wrens as small as dots in twig-like branches, but no wind, since wind carries.

When a moon change happens, when there is a rustle of any kind—a settle of hair, a brightening, a blink—then the air starts up. When it cannot finish, when it lifts but does not land, it hangs. On the Isle of Grief the air drapes on us and we do not part it and we do not leave. Shoulders, lids and arms droop like curtains.

We call our time a day. The sun and moon sit opposite, circles of time and no time. We stay all that day and the next, as possible as birds, our hands opening and closing on captive air.

~

Ed's father was a stevedore offloading fruit from South America on the docks under the eyes of union bosses who were famously tied to the mob. At home he did not say much about this—he worked, he said; he made money—but as time passed he grew less interested in play with his son and less inclined to talk at all. Yet, every week a big cluster of bananas grown downward on a strong stem was brought home and hung in the hall closet to continue ripening for breakfast. It was an old time, an old house, the closet lined in knotty pine and closed off by heavy red curtains filled with dust mites. At the end of a work shift the stevedores took their money to a tavern and got half drunk.

One morning, the father came in weaving and cursing. He bumped against the doorframe and beat the air around his head as though attacked by hornets.

A friend had found, crawling among bananas he'd brought home to his family, a tarantula. The father pulled his WWII trophy machete from its nail on the wall, yanked off the case, threw wide the great curtains and began to hack at the fruit—left, right, down, across, again and again, each stroke more wild, strong and blind, until only the twist-in hook, bent and empty, hung from the ceiling.

The closet was gashed and streaked, the curtains down. Smashed banana dripped everywhere, the hacked skins splayed awkwardly on the floor, sweet stink mixed with sweat and beer and rose, the smoke of a ruined universe.

The mother sat in tears on the dining room floor. The father sank where he was. Ed and the dog just stared.

It was summer then, all that day, and no one there who enjoyed it.

***Notes for a voice-over*:**

They were walking to a movie. "Lucky," they'd said to their friends, "to live so close, to be able to walk there." It was evening as they started, then it began to darken, first in the streets below the buildings, then in the sky.

They were side by side in their coats, the long coats they chose for walking. The air was dark and thick. The thickness of it was fog. They leaned into their stride, pushing air aside and walking through it. Her collar was up against her neck. His scarf and hat nearly met. Chill rubbed on her legs like hands. The circle of what they saw moved with them. The fog made what they saw larger.

A cigarette flared ahead of them. "Move farther out," she whispered. He took her arm and eased closer to the street. Fog made eddies behind them.

In a window, a pull chord dangled, an empty ring at the end. He asked, "What time is it?"

"We're fine," she said.

The air was wet. It sat on their lashes, their cheeks, the tops of their shoes. It swallowed the street behind them. She said, "I could use a cigarette." He was leading with the front of his head. "Pretty close now," he said.

They passed a car splashed with neon. The seats and the seatbacks were split. He asked, "Are you warm enough?" "Yes," she said.

They were walking to a movie. They lived nearby and were able to walk there. It was evening, there was fog. The air was dark and thick. They were side by side in their coats, the long coats they chose for walking. They believed they were nearly there. They should have been there already. They had come to where they might see it. Were it not for the fog, they could have seen it all along.

~

Ed studies the easterly flows for signs of a change.

Weather modeling is practiced by meteorologists and amateurs all over the world, readings taken from instruments placed at any sustainable place; and, as frequently, by a simple turn of the head toward the side not being pelted by rain.

Ed's birthplace at 4:35 a.m. was a room barricaded against the cold November. One of four in the pregnancy, he was the only one who made it. His parents welcomed him with measures of love and grief so arrhythmic he could not reflect them. He imagines there was music, swelling toward him as nourishment, and shapes forming from angles and air. He believes when he first opened his eyes he saw only blue and green, as cats do.

With sunrise, though he cannot explain in exact sentences, he remembers a series of black frames, each with new kinds of growth in them. He wanted to measure and arrange the contents, to look and keep looking for more, sure that something would always be happening inside them.

He was aware of the moon, a lamp near the window, a blanket with his scent from foot to chin. He thought he heard singing near his little cap. The sounds came to him in a separate zone that he would recognize later in the lonesome music of parking garages and the dying transistor in *Apollo 13*. He wanted to know where the sounds came from and felt they could not know who they were without him.

The voices lifted in sweet, soft blend— tenors, altos, sopranos—all sunlit, circling his head like butterflies perhaps imagining him as a strange, sad plant.

An exhaustive outline:

He wasn't going to the war that day or to the glaziers, though a shine took his attentions.

Normally he could see and travel from one island to another. This was also disrupted by the tumbling archduke of someplace, he did not remember where, or the burning of Georgia, he was not sure. When he lifted his nose toward the cumulus, there were clusters of rain, clatters of sword points. His nose flared, a horse lifted. He stumbled, following his eyes to the house where he would fall and be put down.

He was not certain of his ground. Sweat balanced like mercury on his face.

"Perhaps something to eat," he thought. His mother had strained him away to an open plain and he'd grown very, very fast in the surveillance party of milk.

He was sorting the colors of white, looking for tickets or windshields or the right not to die in his dreams and varying times of the day. His kiss glanced off his breath as a house blew by, the carpet of wind alive with what he'd learned of serpents. Shrapnel laced exquisite lines in his flesh. The moss at the creek bed fled from him, hurrying northward—Alaska. Mars. Less, not more was needed, by token or touring car.

Soup boiled, the engine seized, a paper slipped from the desk to the floor like a boa. He was surrounded by a series of lost phrases. What could he say to the steeplejack hanging the last of his family on the house front? Stop? A spoon shook under his mouth. He saw a beatitude of cats.

An amalgam of all his minutes forced itself from his throat like the plume from the Carpathian scanning the cold studded sea.

~

Ed terrorizes the goldfish by peering at it close up with his two great eyes. As he moves away from the tank, he spots a spider running back to the molding. He smashes it with his shoe then sidesteps his cat, ignoring its plaintive mew as it seeks to brush the legs of the living. But he is weary of providing these lessons on the Deity.

He ejects *Things to Come* when Dr. Harding tells his daughter that nothing anymore will make anyone comfortable.

A dry air mass has riddled the carpet with static.

He touches metal to ground himself. As if he had not looked through the window thousands of times before with the same result, he looks again, searching for contrast or a small bird.

A low pressure system is bringing more snow. The grey weight of it rolls in. He retreats to the DVD shelf and selects his go-to films, his reliable sled dogs, restless and biting the gang line: "mush, *Vertigo*; mush, *Scarface*; mush, *Three Days of the Condor*."

If he is in the mood after that, "mush, *Big Fish*."

Or, he ventures coyly as the refrigerator drops a load of ice, he might just try a new release, something still in its plastic, and play only the alternate ending.

He is so tired of himself.

The furnace breathes heavily. He steps sideways to straddle the vent. Now he can't move away.

Notes for framing a small scene:

It is not Chinese though it is the color of oxblood. It is a red Chinese table lamp that sits on a small, scrolled table in the dining room.

His hand on the table, three of his fingers forming a contemplative tent, Bill looks up, but not at the narrator of the scene who in the meantime has penciled "…" into his script.

Uncertain what he is supposed to be saying, Bill touches the deep red porcelain to get his bearings. Receiving only silence, he sighs toward someone out of camera range, picks up his drink and walks out to the sun porch.

The plot started out with a thread about randy field nasturtiums but soon approached the trichinoid or other means of advancing disease through dirt. The crawling sensations it gave the narrator were pleasurable, reminiscent of early adventures in the grass, sensations he would not feel in a similarly structured piece depicting large armies advancing on small towns. The narrator wonders if he would ever feel that again, if that expression were still in him—if not, how could he return to the story line? He thinks.

Amy, the set-up indicates, is not part of Bill's life anymore, though she had been for quite awhile, and when she left, she left him looking for another way to mark time. She also left a red table lamp.

She is not greatly missed, not on a par with food and shelter and card games, does not raise the prickly hairs of immediate pain like the wanton violin crying out the higher notes next door. But on a small table in the dining room the red table lamp sits, famous and alone, where Bill can turn it on or off as he likes. He looks at it every day. It could be that he loves it.

The narrator wonders if he should write in a dog? A house cricket?

At times he has difficulty distinguishing 'swallow' from 'wallow,' though it does not curb his enjoyment at wrinkling the plot.

There are two narrators, of course, there always are, one reading aloud, one changing the other with notes.

How bored is this one? Enough to topple kingdoms or abandon linear flow? He always has the house staff to fall back on should things go badly: one to do for him, one to do, one to do him in. He turns his attention back to the story—action is starting up again.

Three men have come down the corridor to meet Bill on the porch. One had an accident with his knee in the dark dining room, indicated by his cursing and rubbing as he catches up.

"Should have switched on the lamp!" the narrator notes in the column.

"Didn't see one, it was dark!" the wounded fellow retorts.

"Hopefully you didn't break anything, except maybe your leg," Bill says companionably.

But in the background, from the dining room, they begin to notice a rocking sound, the rocking and tipping of a bumped table, back and forth in longer and more dangerous intervals, the tick-tock of a table turned into the metronome of disaster.

Finally the tip is too great and something crashes to the floor.

Everyone holds his breath, waiting for the next sound: the crash of porcelain, the shatter of oxblood.

Nothing.

Then one of the men, suddenly brightening, exclaims, "The

other table!"

Everyone applauds, charmed, proud and relieved.

~

Who could Ed stand to love in this snow-bank? With whom could he wait out the Storm of the Century? He does not miss his first wife, who is dead, or the second, or those others unwed but lost just the same; does not miss the excited beginnings, the desperate, delicious attractions, the predictable violence he eventually enacts to reestablish himself—just as he does not miss radio, though he pretends to. Nor does he remember whether the women were beautiful and calm or spicy and dangerous. He does remember sun like golden oil on their legs, and fine blond down on their delicate arms.

Crystals of ice are forming under the snow pack, none of them into recognizable words.

Throughout a life of observation and description, he has trained himself to remember all he's ever said and done, but when he plays it back he finds nothing new. He takes up the remote to increase the sound.

It is not true, he now knows, that water draining in a sink rotates one way in the northern hemisphere, the reverse in the south. Life glorifies the Coriolis Effect. He rotates with the earth, which means he will not fall off and neither will his thoughts which, like gravity, he cannot see though they persist in a kind of invisible curiosity museum.

~

Icicles the length of tire irons hang over the porch.

He moves to another room as if showing someone: "This is my study. This is my desk, my picture by Caspar David Friedrich—you anticipated which one it would be.

"This is my computer."

He has not checked his email in two weeks. He wants instead to wait until all of a sudden he feels he must check it, must without fail, check or forfeit his life.

When that happens, when he is so summoned, he knows he will find great, glittering gems, messages of stunning importance, lines of significance beyond anything he could ever expect on this earth—words and pictures larger and more encompassing than the stratosphere; brighter and hotter than the outline of the sun; more inspiring and shattering than the images held deep down in the bellies of cameras lost in the darkest pockets of space.

"This is my bedroom…."

Notes re: The Lorelei, rocks, doom, etc.

She speaks quietly of herself in conversation. She desires want. She wants desire. Desire wants her. She is, in a moment, everything and the moment itself.

Through gauzed confusions she culls, slides and murmurs a story of herself in history. Smoke trails a lip, an ear. She steps her men down slowly through their imagined homes—the halls, the rooms, the chambers of enchantment, the caverns, the hills of their youth.

see: Clara and Brahms.
Emily alone.
Wagner and his young king.
The serpentine Cleopatra.

***A flashback*:**

A man stands on the veranda. The veranda is grand and white and beautiful and people at the party call it a pavilion, though it is not. They look out at the beautiful veranda and see a man at the outlook of a pavilion. They believe they are thinking of the view and not of sex.

The pavilion has vertical pieces where a hand might rest, a peaked roof of beams and glass. Below is lattice. Everything complicates itself, up and down.

Through the outlook is the night, divided into sky and sea. The night sky and the sea at night are so beautiful that verandas overlooking them are pavilions. All of the colors in the sky and the sea are blue—lapis, peacock, marine and blue so blue as to be black.

The guests hold glasses shaped like diamonds. They look up as a man arrives and say, "Oh!" or, "There you are!" and one says, "I'm mixing another batch. Have a seat!" The man sits down beside a woman with a sharp chin. He says, "May I?" She crosses her legs and leans toward him and says, "Possibly," and someone else laughs.

The laughter is as sharp as her chin, as the points her knees make, as the angles of their glasses, the tip of the pavilion, the fumes of the gin in a new batch. The man flourishes his handkerchief. "A Houdini!" someone says. The man dabs at the corners of his eyes.

The woman watches him and thinks, "such beautiful blue eyes," then looks away toward the wall of glass. She rises and crosses the room to the outside.

A man stands on the veranda. He feels it is a pavilion, but it is not, though it is beautiful. People look out and see a man at the outlook of a pavilion. They believe they are thinking of the view.

The woman steps out and joins him. His cigarette responds to a breeze, his fingers hook lattice. She leans against him, light as a sheet. All the colors in the sky and sea are blue.

~

Ed knows he will go outside again, and not just for shoveling. Surrounding his house is everything else entirely, and he must go out or be crushed by its mass. It is just the snow.

He will go out, though winter has hidden the world so well he can't imagine how far he would have to travel to find it. He will go out, though in these remaining nights of lock-down he curls in his bed like Death's scythe, pillows and quilts platooned around him. Coyotes, raptors and future ex-wives roam the perimeter.

He is hard to find, even for himself, but he will emerge. It is just the weather.

One day he will go somewhere, though just now the possibility dries between his lids. He folds like a jackknife. Nothing and nothing more take shape in him. The clock pulls relentlessly at the nets for sleeping and the nets for failing to sleep. It is just winter.

He sets up his back-up portable weather station with battery power system, wireless transceiver and sensor tripod mast to monitor for signs of a thaw. What it shows him is winter.

He knows that spring will come, babbling and strewing flowers, whatever it is said to do, and he will be ready. He will go out among the crocuses, wave at neighbors, take a drive, go for tacos and beer, peruse the bar, go swimming or dancing in shoes without socks—all those things.

But just now he is as lonely as a small civet.

He leaves the blinds down and imagines color.

To exercise leg and voice, he escorts Hope on yet another tour of his house as if offering it for sale: "This is the kitchen. This is the dining room. There is room for a table for eight, these plants make it look smaller. They're inside so they won't freeze outdoors in their pots.

"This is the hallway and this is the coat closet. Notice the open ceilings. This is the living room, and . . . wait, let me turn down the music. It's 'The Messiah.' Do you like it?"

Notes from a dream of the outside:

A man steps onto a bus idling in a narrow stall. Children make soft slapping sounds on the windows.

A man bends into a taxi at a yellow stand. The engine makes soft tapping sounds under the hood.

A man walks onto the pier where there is a large white ship sailing today to Maui. Water makes soft lapping sounds at its sides.

A breeze nudges his clothes, his ankles and wrists. It raises his skin. The sun looks like a mango or an orange. Stewards on the ship go up the ladders and in a hatch as though drawn through a straw.

A woman arrives at the pier. Her sandals make soft clapping sounds on the wood. She sees him look at what he sees: a large white ship; sees his suit wave on him like a flag. "Maui," she says to him and looks down the pier. "Maui," he says and nods. They see men on the decks with manageable loads. She moves on down the pier. He leans with a breeze.

Children pour from a yellow bus. They make parentheses and run around him. A dog makes high yapping sounds on its leash.

Taxis, cars, and people swirl in. Cameras leap from pockets, lunches spill. Couples turn. Someone bumps his wallet. A woman pats her hair. He smells popcorn. The pier fills with litter, with departing noise as from a train. He makes an O in space.

Then tickets flash, stubs flutter, cameras close, banners coil, voices wilt, the pier empties. Passengers go to the ship, up the ladders and in a hatch as though drawn through a straw. Water churns at the stern.

The man thinks "Maui" to himself, and nods. There is a breeze. Then he turns back toward the city. He bends into a taxi, steps onto a bus. He resumes his bed. His mouth makes soft napping sounds in his sleep.

~

Notes on travel and a kind of self-loathing:

It was hot where they were and they were unable to escape it. Layers slipped in their up-white-breaking and down-green-declining breaths. They could hardly do anything. The air their animal blood had nourished so faithfully paused at the ledges and would not jump.

It was hot where they were, inside and outside the same. As if hot were wanted, as if it were offered as meals. As if hot were the sleeve of the way to Pension Anna.

Welcome swelled out to them, opening, closing the doors of commerce. They'd brought their valise of describable deeds. They had and had not reserved rooms. They kept and were kept; mostly they kept to themselves, covering a vase and a mirror with scarves. Things they thought of when they thought of themselves were portable. The weather they believed in was carried with them.

They were arranged-for like pets and rounded ever more toward the center, the ballroom of limited choice. There they beamed on their axis and stayed longer than can be imagined, the concierge, familiar and filled with mirth, showing, rewinding and showing them films of interminable loss.

~

Ed opens the door to the porch. It is April. The green points sent out from bulbs are drilling their way upward through still-frozen ground.

He leaves a foot inside as one arm holds the screen door out like a shield.

Low sunlight strokes his cheek from ear to chin. He waits for it to kiss him sufficiently awake. When he has waited long enough, when his white body is one with the remaining chill, he backs into the house, closing the screen behind him like the cover of a tall book.

The Jewel Encrusted Alligator

Any little thing is water.

Gertrude Stein,
"Tender Buttons"

Her first husband was trained in reconnaissance, so getting loose of him had not been easy, his last maneuver employing an accomplice to take all of her collectibles from the house—for she was a devoted collector—and sell them in his shop. To be fair, he offered each of her art prints, etchings, marbles, miniature totem poles and Pre-Columbian clay heads back to her for half the retail price (that discount her allotment by marriage), providing she could get to the items before they were sold.

"Nothing personal," he said. Everything is personal.

Thrown back on her roots, she thought to dedicate herself to finding again what had been happily sought and so quickly lost—consoled by the hope of better representatives of everything. The next husband, for example, though he would not live forever, must be an improvement.

The result is a story of acquisition and loss, as all stories are, told in Time, which is not as straightforward as we like to think.

This particular day, for instance, several and many months after that particular day, in her house on Ravenna Boulevard, when returning from the phone that interrupted her laundry she enters the room and looks at the ironing board then stops dead still— the blue cotton shirt flaccid on the board, the arm dangling as if in swoon from a fainting couch—suddenly her life feels foreign and unbearable for no discernible reason based in the present.

She goes for a walk, ultimately swinging by Goodwill where (and why not) there might be something familiar and alluring to recover from abandonment and keep.

Other days, strolling out from under the lace leaf maples and into the fields of the estate she visits from time to time, the yellow jackets investigating her hair, the air deliberating its next move, the quails clucking at magpies dragging their long tails over mowed-down wheat—in such moments there may be a feeling of patience and abundance as in the recollection of finely played music. And then the deer may be there.

She never sees them advance, the dozen or so adolescents who have in mind a patch beyond her. Loose and insolent, white tails up, they assess her and her conflicted dog who alternately jumps up and sits. By increments and charades of indifference they settle into watchful standing.

All this is in the literature of the world.

The afternoon gathers like a caterpillar.

She pulls a thistle from the lawn and calls the dog by its name.

The sun in sequent rings moves to another place. So do the deer.

The dog snaps at a fly. A bee picks out something it likes.

A whole day goes by.

Earlier summers, in Utah, on weekends, the days when things usually happen, she might be enticed by a turned wood and buckskin chair on the porch and, discovering it to be unexpectedly comfortable, fall suddenly asleep and stay that way until a breeze finds her.

That afternoon the sun had lain on her cheek so silently and so long it too had dozed and she hesitated to stir it or herself. More influenced by a change in the air, however, she rose to take a ride down the strip and out beyond the rise.

Soon a thunderstorm appeared, wandering across a plain of low relief, picking its way toward the Great Salt Lake, the place where imaginations go to die.

She had practiced reading the earth—a desiccated coyote; a bramble tall enough to grab her leg and hold on; the stirred-up dust singing in her wet hair: all signs indicated it was time to head back. She flicked a rein.

The horse turned as if yanked. She gripped the pommel and held on, the animal galloping the route it knew best of them all, finally stopping abruptly in a tumble of dust, sweat and alarm at the place in the fence where it knew it should be able to enter.

She had to lean very, very far forward along its neck to unhitch the gate. In passing, their eyes slowed down and looked into each other, close-up.

The next step was to say nothing.

~

In the photo there are four people holding up an oil painting. Perhaps it is a gift, a find or a clue; a memory or a burden. Each holds a corner, steadying it for the camera. The sun cuts their faces in half. They appear to be in hot weather and the oil looks sticky.

The four want to draw our attention to the painting and so we look. First apparent are three pale green trees in the foreground where the painter has hinted at remnant sun both there and on the edge of the river. That lower lit corner is, in relation to the rest, a negative.

Coming out from the left is the black river, cutting into the forest, darkening, looking bigger and more full of purpose as it goes. Across the river to the right is one layer after another of dark trees marching away from the water and up a hill. It could be that there is no hill at all but trees that happen to grow in pattern—but we are meant to believe there is a hill and on it the trees are so thick and close we do not see their cones (for they are evergreens in a northern clime) nor any animals or birds. Neither can we see the trunks or any uncovered ground, only a feathered mass. Such trees do not have to lie down to weigh on you.

If one were to diagram this painting, there would be several lines, labels, indices, values and elevations, but only one color, plus black.

Above the presumed hill is a green aurora borealis that touches the trees in a thrilling way and intermingles with their tops. The sense of where the sky lifts up or touches down is vague; and maybe, after all, it is instead a portrait of a green forest fire blazing up through the top of the picture and out by the edges and sure to march downriver this way.

One of the people in the photo has gout, one is a neighbor standing at a kind of attention and one has an earnest but failing heart. The woman on the right seems to be tired of holding up her end of the painting, perhaps worrying she will die alone with it.

~

She grew up half a mile from a family of three children who had no chins. It was like playing with the dead: their mouths, never with much of anything to say, sank right into their necks.

They had talent. When one of them turned into the bright sun his eyes closed. When one shouted upwind no one heard it. When one lay too long on the warm grass after lunch he stopped moving altogether and then, after a bit, got up again. Magic.

At the end of a day there, the hours filled with nothing but enough, to avoid the busy road home she angled across 5th Street and cut through the Anderson's yard, skipped through an alley and dashed into a forest so small it was called a wood.

Eventually she reached the big rock. A little further, at the salmon berry bush, she would see the neighbor's house and the trailer with the old man and then she would be mostly home.

Suddenly a bird shrieked at her, flapped wildly and shrieked again, louder, longer and closer.

Terror tore through her like a steam whistle. She flew more than ran the rest of the way—through the gap in the fence and beyond into her yard and around the shed with its spiders and sprays, swinging wide to avoid the arbor and the green-red tangle of roses that all summer had grown taller and taller, reaching their sticky green fingers up toward the windows at the back of the house.

~

One story of Weeping Buddha is that he weeps for the troubles of the world, absorbing the common grief. The world is profoundly sad and someone must always weep for its sorrows so the rest of us can be joyful.

Some refer to his meditative posture—a rolled-up version of sitting such as the one the hedgehog adopts when startled—as a way to open and activate the third eye.

It is also said, but not in a convincing way, that the pose is for the benefit of apprentice carvers who must first learn the form of the body before practicing the face—as students of human dissection must work on the hands, the feet, the torso of the cadaver or confront too soon, too nakedly, the gateway to the human, the stilled muscles of facial expression.

An alternate story goes this way: Two warriors confront each other in numerous battles, each time wearing a mask. After many such encounters in which neither had seen the other's face, the older warrior kills the younger. Upon removing the mask of the vanquished, he discovers it is his own lost son. He folds forward in sorrow.

If you touch Weeping Buddha, your own sadness is supposed to pass into him.

In surprising places like Germany, hidden behind a Japanese style fence and gate, one may be strolling the Weeping Willow Allee and encounter the Buddha between the peony beds and other specialty plants.

Flags of battle in the time of masks were nearly as big

as the horses. The unbroken field, the looming violence, the crackling of saddles and tendons all combined to create great winds that snapped and tore at the banners, pulling the standard bearers hard aside. It took all their hands to hold on.

The eyes of the horses were huge and white.

Without a battle, the rending of flags and the fright of the mounts might still decide something.

The reverse figure is Hotei, or Laughing Buddha, whose stomach may be rubbed for good luck. Luck is not the opposite of sadness but similar to it, as death is to swamp weeds for a mallard.

~

One bright day in the International District she purchases a tiny Weeping Buddha. Before handing it back to her, the clerk drops it into a gold net bag with drawstring.

Taken by the fluidity of the gesture and the elegance of the container, she purchases a dozen such bags and sets about collecting items to fit them—a miniature beer stein inscribed *Eric*, a tiny book covered with Hokusai's Wave, the cast of an Early Pliocene mandible, etc. — dropping each into its own bag, and drawing the string.

Once tight in their sacks, the objects slept quietly like cats and puppies, dreaming the active and comforting scenes of dependent animals who know nothing about the trip to the river.

~

The horse in Utah is named Champ, the dog that is seldom seen, Lady.

~

She names all her cats after Salo, Kurt Vonnegut's Tralfamadorian, an emissary from a race of ancients on another planet who live all the times of their lives simultaneously: past, future, and an elaborately wide and punctuated present.

Weeping Buddha curls forward, his palms coaxing the shaved head down closer and closer to his heart.

~

At the birthday party, she greets her old friend in the hallway. The friend has brought her new husband with her. The husband laughs merrily in response to "Welcome! Dinner is almost ready!" He is warm and expansive and has an invitingly round stomach which he pats, anticipating a feast. "Lucky we got here in time," he says.

When he later sits dying on the edge of his bed, his head down, his back rounding and leaning, he says to his wife who holds him in the hammock of her arms that he feels funny; using her breath as his own gives out and taking it with him.

~

On the first night of the class in Modern American Poetry, the professor asks his graduate students to stand and read from their work to show the freshmen how it is to be done.

Rather than write like a graduate student she takes up

the Course Catalog again, this time circling *Anthropology* — a discipline, she reads, with many practical applications.

In class she learns that captains of the Alaskan halibut fleets create their own languages to keep the hot fishing spots secret . . . that the data of culture and social life are susceptible to exact scientific treatment . . . that bands or ligaments connect different elements of the anthropoid ape into a movable machinery … that early scholars believed a "vital force" resided in enzymes, at the same time discounting primitive belief in the magical nature of tools … that a number of arguments seems to prove the soul is eternal and indestructible and has existed for all eternity … that the palmaris longis, a muscle in the middle of the human wrist, is sometimes fully developed and sometimes not there at all … that Livingstone's bearers said, at their first-ever glimpse of the sea: "We marched along with our father, believing that what the ancients had always told us was true, that the world had no end; but all at once, the world said to us, *I am finished: there is no more of me.*"

And something about allometry and chi-squares.

She nails a 4-inch halibut jig above her desk next to the utility knife of a kind made in Finland for at least the last 1,000 years, a knife with a reach for surprise sticking—hers, with a detailed handle depicting a horse head, hangs in a hand-tooled leather sheath with curved tip.

She can't believe her good fortune in only the third quarter of school to chance upon an auction not just of older horse head knives, but two other styles unknown to her: Hirvikoirapuukko, the wolf head; Ajokoirapuukko, the hound.

The miniature set of dominoes that no one else bid for she arranges on a small table—fitting each piece close together and steadily adding to form the outward spiral of an ammonite.

She can hardly wait for her second year.

Next to the bust of Neanderthal in the living room, using pins and black boxes with Plexiglas lids, she makes artful arrangements of pot and vase designs amid etchings of Etruscan towns.

In the dining room she hangs the 1940's print of a wolf on a snowy hill overlooking a sleeping town—tracks behind, village ahead, the hot animal breath; lights out below, the horses in.

"Things can disappear," she tells Salo, recounting a lesson, "when you stop looking at them."

~

All her cats have the same name for her, though which it is, among the rich variety of sounds they make, she cannot tell.

~

One husband by now is long gone, dead, in fact, and she has lucked into a far better example. The world demonstrates a pulling effect; one equinox, for instance, signals another that it is next up.

One day she is telling the neighbor's grandchildren the story of the three little boats. The first one was fiberglass and too light, the second was wood and too much work, the third was bigger but not quite as comfortable as the second which in their hearts had been, after all, in retrospect and considering everything, just right.

"Do you ever sleep on a boat?" they ask.

"Yes."

"Is it nice? Even at night?"

"Yes," she replies, "it can be like being rocked to sleep, back and forth, gently back and forth. It is very nice."

It is like being in the palm of the sea when the sea has shape. And when the boat is lured too far from the slip the lines catch with a reassuring soft tug and bring it back.

But for those sleeping outside the port, those who rest at the ends of long chains, whose anchors slip in the action of wake and tides and lose hold, then there is only the dark in all directions.

"Snacks!" the mother calls from the kitchen. The children lift like gulls and, like gulls, drop into chairs—legs first, then wings.

"See," says the tallest, the one who can look down into her glass without spilling. "My cookie floats like a boat!" She hovers as if to launch, weight all forward on two small hands.

~

Mornings, dew on the deck keeps them below with coffee in the galley. The phosphor of the moonlit night is once again invisible and the blue herons leave for their secret places, feet dripping wet sentences on the pier. He backs the boat from its berth and slips it outbound, a "V" through the water of their spare time.

An osprey swings low and looks in. The water has lain

down flat, drawing its fingers along the hull, tasting it, listening idly for news. They drift to where the fish might be: in the confluence of small rips.

The Sound begs them to stare, tempts them with softened lines and blurred definitional points, with coy circles in what passes for the lee.

They respond as they know how: propping their feet on ladders and rails, oiling and exposing their necks, talking in short sentences and squinting far out to where something at some point might happen. It would have to be self-fulfilling, whatever else it might be; potentials run at boat length and they are midships. It is that way with them on boats.

~

In other earlier years she would run three miles a day and bicycle five, pick at her grainy meals, adrenalize herself for studies—busyness, not peace, as the former is the word of present tense.

When the cat goes out one night and fails to return he takes all the good ideas with him.

She goes to the door.

Listening, she hears a loggerhead shrike knife through the shrubby steppes in the shadows of Cedar Breaks.

Holding the cold handle, she feels the anchor cable sticking up from humus to trail into the peaty murk of Arbor Lake. A *dead man*, they call it; the drowned end of earthly coil.

Looking out, she sees waves of people with rags and masks climbing the crisscross legs of the rigs—the masts of the oil fields of the Caucasus, source and appetite of the great engines.

Over the rooftop chimneys, the silhouettes of trees seem to be waving for help.

~

The whistle of the Burlington Northern slips through their window as the train snakes along the water, carrying what it declares to be important but is only asleep.

Further on, the engine will bend east toward Chicago, sounding its horn at intersections all across Montana. Passengers roll like ball bearings in their berths, wrapped in the lonely sounds they think are their own, dreaming of arrival in different, happier places.

As the train wanders away, its vibrations stay behind and travel from the wheels through the iron spikes grounding the rails and down into the trucked-in rock of the rail bed. From there it radiates through the permeable and one arm of it wriggles through glacial till until it finally reaches the foundations of their home, which, though confident and sturdy, shudders slightly. Inside, the two of them sleep the sleep of the communicant.

~

She had not been fast enough in those terrible old days, had failed to get to that store in time to retrieve enough and so she no longer has the 1960's wooden replica of Brancusi's "The Kiss" or the tourist-trade totem pole with wings or the Modigliani print or the marbles from

Bennington Forge. And of her classical LPs, everything is missing from T through W—Tchaikovsky through "The Ring."

~

The best marbles are the German Sulphides, large and clear with an animal inside; in her prized example, a fish. Not one of the workhorses such as the Cat's Eye, Aggie, Glassie, Purey or Pee-Wee, it commonly resides on shelves next to books.

Everything to do with the game of marbles is round, deep, hard or human. Generally it is played in a ring that resembles Earth.

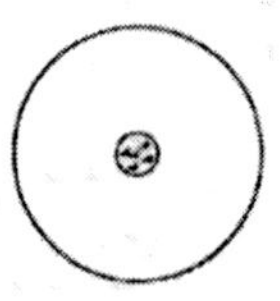

"Fen Clearance!" is a tactical shout to stop a player clearing debris from his shot; "Fen Burying!" warns him from stomping your shooter into the dirt.

The game also may be played with holes or against a wall.

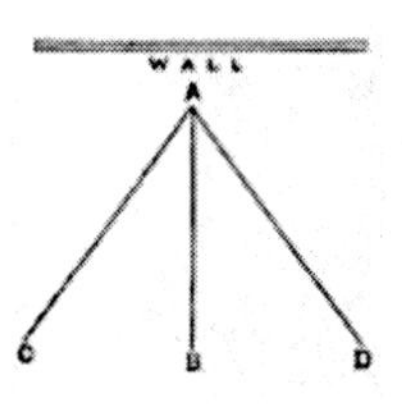

Hunching is not allowed; hoisting, sometimes. You must lag to start.

The ring-tailed lemur occupies geographical ranges that at least partially overlap nine other primates: the red-tailed and white-tailed sportive lemurs; the brown, the greater, the fat-tailed dwarf lemurs; the ruffed and lesser bamboo lemurs; the aye-aye and sifaka.

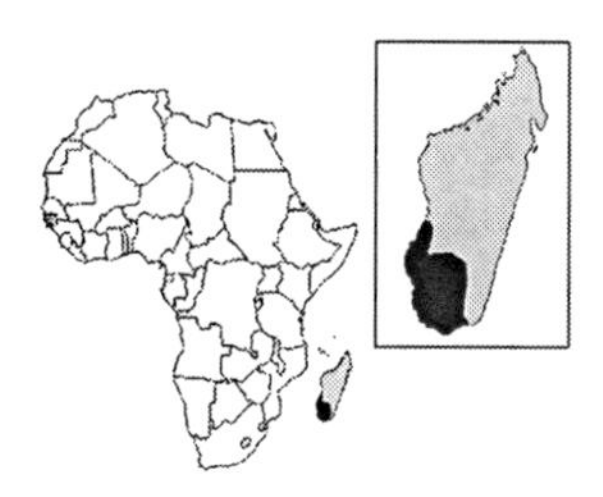

In 1610 Galileo Galilei described the rings of Saturn as ears and handles. A few years later Christiaan Huygens called them disks.

There are seven rings made up of millions of moonlets orbiting loosely together. You can see the stars through them.

We represent them by letters A through G.

A, B, C, D, E, F, G

At the Ring of Kerry all goes well but in Scotland as they reach the steep pull on to Beinn Liath Mhor's east top, they are plagued by swarms of midges and fierce storms come were upon them. She hears a weird humming sound from her trekking pole then sees a massive flash and feels a heavy thump on the handle and sharp pain at the back of her head. There follows deafening thunder and torrential rain.

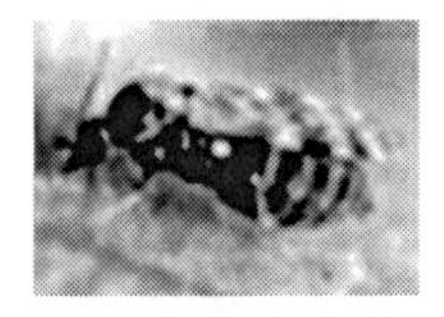

An Adult Midge

By themselves, the few baskets of yams on the beach are just a few baskets of yams. Science.

~

It is a white room and good light comes in.

It is a white room and good light comes in and, by oblique sound, a bird.

It is a white room and good light comes in and, by oblique sound, a bird and then omnivorous night.

Limbs and linens; the confusion of the senses by skin; Glenmorangie, Glengoyne; Il Dulce Gusto. The harmonies of the keys of the ocean—these too are things to be collected—the lidded, the unlidded eye; Amun-Ra; the sounds that scatter beasts.

~

Sculpting *Homo habilensis* is similar to carving a totem pole or moai only not in wood or living stone but lumped clay and copied from fragments not from old drawings of hillsides filled with ferns and berries. You need not take two million years to do it. For *Homo rudolfensis,* add the cigarette that trails smoke into the eye you partially close in squint.

One day four violent knocks erupt on the door. Salo cowers against a wall, his furry back a tent. She peeks through the peephole to see what is easily the biggest man she has ever seen. His uniform has to stretch continental distances to hold on. Because it appears to be a policeman, she opens the door.

He is all creak and leather. One hand rides his holster the way a careful rider might sit on the rail before entering the corral.

"Do you know the tenants upstairs?" he asks, his voice further pinning the cat.

"No," she says. He only waits.

"No," she says again, "I don't know anyone up there. Just a minute, my cat is freaking out. Let me step outside." She smiles disarmingly and pulls the door shut. "You're not after the cat, are you?"

He shifts; that is, one hip cocks up and all the weight comes off the opposite leg which bends. His hands come together at the buckle, thumbs hooked on the belt. He gives off a musty smell.

"I have a warrant," he says. "Have they moved out?"

Guilt dances on her face. Her mind replays the steady treadmill rhythms she hears from there sometimes; the scooted chair, the slammed refrigerator door. Evidence.

"Maybe the Office can help," she offers. She points across the commons and retreats inside. Splitting the blinds, she watches the last of him lumber under the trees, his heavy footsteps grinding into the walk.

"Wow, Salo," she says, as the cat straightens, "who would believe that?"

The doorbell rings.

She sneaks back to the peephole to see a young man wearing a "Census Taker" badge. His body addresses the door but his face is turned with interest toward the trees and the echo of retreating tread.

"Let's not," she whispers to the cat as she leaves her post, "let's just not."

~

By now she has a second dead husband and in many ways is becoming like him: She has candies in her pocket. She is older than she was. She has a favorite cup. She has written a sentence and changed it. She is a plain book.

Her friend writes: *Do you remember that closed-up house—overgrown—we had to fight our way to the front window—a small house—and inside, well, we couldn't see all the way in, but we could make out that huge desk—all cubbyholes and small drawers—piled high with papers? I wondered then as I do now how anyone could have left it.*

It is hard exactly to remember loss.

Sometimes the dead animal does not, after all, turn toward you and open its eyes. Or in the absolute of the silent dark dream when ground dissolves and you float, suddenly a noise or light renews the world—but sloppily and without key elements.

Sometimes a sinkhole opens in the chest or there is a

slippage of geologic plates; or lines unravel from cleats; or pieces of something clink and echo all the way down the cistern that is only half-full.

Sometimes you hear the hammering of wind and rain and, sometimes, there is simply nothing, then more and more of it.

~

In secondhand stores she heads straight for the bins of pictures, searching for the brown ink etching sold all those years ago before she could buy it back for half price.

She has described it often to dealers and friends: "It has a cascading creek of good size, trees, a lot of fine detail, a sky with clouds you wouldn't call *scudding*. There are no animals, but a log across the water" (she was not sure it went all the way across) "and it's old, maybe as much as 100 years old, and not signed but probably done by an outdoorsman—a fisherman or hunter—because of the way the rocks were handled: dangerous-looking for wet feet and no good for sitting, though maybe that is why the log was there even if it didn't go all the way across.

"It is in a brown wood frame with no wire so it has to lean against the wall, propped by a vase. *Have you seen it?"*

The person who gave it to her had cancer and died. He had begun to believe at the end that cancer is the new Purgatory.

Dante thought Purgatory a mountain in the south. Rome calls it a condition of existence.

Maybe cancer is a purging fire that looks for the voids

in our faithful souls (which, though precisely informed as they can be, are riddled) and there, within sight of the holy poets, takes up its wild and replicate ways.

~

Salo spots and freezes a bird in the thicket.

~

Champ raises up on two legs.

~

The Buddha has been in the same position so long he can no longer unfold to see us.

~

Do you hear the birds saying goodnight, Salo? Do you think they sing for you? Where are you on the time-space continuum when you stretch out your long, furry body? Do you remember things?

There are oddities in the world and one of them is that we keep on with no idea how it will be. What sort of plan is that? Sometimes a breeze (we can call it conversation, if you know what that is) is all we need for assurance and sometimes there is unrelenting rain.

You aren't just any one thing, Salo, do you know that? You are as variable and elaborate as anything in nature and art; as unique as teeth and ears and prints. If you were a recently uncovered habitation site—well, never mind. Just keep sifting for dangers with that mammalian brain of yours. Your favorite collar may help, and there's the past, too, if you can draw on it. I won't even bring up parallel universes.

All the inattentive birds in the world cannot obliterate boredom, Salo. Avoid it, and that other sad thing, the thing we haven't talked about yet, that thing I know about and you don't ... but it's a lovely night tonight, out here under the stars, so even though Orion points his bow in the direction of someone we know and fits the arrow he will not be able to retract, I am not going to tell it to you.

~

Where she is living now, in a place unlike any she has lived in before or anywhere she would choose if she could from among them all—a conclusion that eludes her—it is warm and pleasant and not particularly thrilling though her heart seems to work at this elevation as well as at any, which is the pride and pity of hearts everywhere when they get together.

~

On vacation she enters a secondhand store and there sees a picture, the best of all the Maxfield Parrish prints and just like the one sold out from under her way back then.

It had been a gift: *Daybreak* had hung in her friend's living room against the yellowed cream wall, depicting within its antique frame and under its smoke-smudged glass two stilled lives that radiate curves of color and soft, impossible glows. There are tall classical columns, of course, it is of that era, and fresh-leafed trees and soon, it tells us, in the delicacy of a fine new day, one slight being will bend to kiss the other awake. All the images prepare us for a sweet conjunction.

She picks it up eagerly, but as she turns it this way and that, she worries. Is the frame really gesso or have the corners been built up to look old?

Is this an original print or a laser copy? Is some of the margin missing from the right? Does she sense a difference in hue? Is that a signature or a stamp? The wire is not new, the glass not wavy....

Why isn't it tinged with smoke?

She could weep.

~

In the movie the girl cannot open the gate, the boat drifts into shipping lanes, the cat dies poisoned under the porch

~

At the free symphony concert that begins all musical seasons, before the conductor steps on stage, she hears a particular kind of rustling. She looks up from where she is sitting to see a small group of nuns enter the aisle opposite, habits sweeping side to side like long, black hair. As they turn to sit she notices that only the surface fabric is black, black over very dark blue and, of course, white. They settle, magmas of cloth overflowing the armrests.

She hardly ever sees nuns inside a building. Most often she encounters them on sidewalks, moved as much by wind as by themselves, their eyes cast down, hands hidden—the forms that constancy pins its hopes on.

As the group arranges their folds, a wooden bead clacks briefly on metal once, once again—discreet as only the beads of a nun can be.

She remembers that she too is wearing a uniform and in a conversational gesture reaches up to feel the secure gold chain at her neck from which a gold cap holds, as surely as once did the gums, the incisor of a chimpanzee.

~

What does a fossil cost? A bog? The bead of a nun? What is the life of things? Are three quart-size Ball canning jars with tin lids filled with pre-1960 marbles enough?

Having dropped her car at the Valet service too early to meet her friends for the movie, she wanders into the gift shop of the Davenport Hotel. She has twenty minutes to kill and a little bit of money. Picking up a box of Altoids, her attention is caught by a shiny display of pillboxes, candle snuffers, and filigree-rimmed mirrors.

Just then the porter pushes a cart of baggage in from the drive-around. As he charges through the automatic doors a shock of wind blows in with him, ruffles the papers at the check-in desk, laces over the bronze statue of a man on a bench reading a newspaper, and slides into the shop.

The doors swing closed again, the air stills.

In the display sits an item she has never before encountered; or if she had seen one, she'd never properly considered it—bright, alluring, foreign, gaudy, cold, novel, garish, unique, repellent, interesting.

It catches her breath unreasonably. What on earth is it for? When she reaches for it she feels as if she is reaching into the cosmos.

She picks it up, turns it over, counts the faux emeralds that run down the lines of its spine, rubs the phony rubies of its eyes, tests its heft, opens the hinged jaws of the compartment too shallow to hold anything. She's not sure she likes it. She doesn't want to leave it behind.

A small piece of unfinished edge tears into her thumb. She bleeds big dark drops onto the lid of a white box.

What good, she asks herself, a reddening tissue tight against the wound, could this possibly be? Are there more of them?

Once again the automatic doors slap open. A road-rumpled family wanders into the lobby, stretching happily, spilling Cokes and bits of Cheezits on the carpet while their Durango is driven to the garage.

As the doors close, so does an internal argument. She hands over the last of her cash. The clerk drops into a gold net bag with drawstring the receipt, the box of mints and the jewel encrusted alligator.

A Partial View Toward Nazareth

. . . the horizon of the unknown moves together with the horizon of science and is never dispelled by it

I.P. Culiano
from "Out of this World"

Traffic Patterns

At 3rd and Division, as she idles at the light, she notices in her periphery that two full lanes of cars have quietly appeared alongside on the right, kept from her own lane by a parallel fence of concrete wedges. Where have they come from? Why do they have their own light?

At her green she creeps forward in a cautious low gear. The two lanes to her left accompany her; on the other side the isolated fourth and, she sees now, a fifth is held back. Then, gradually, she sees that the far left lane has disappeared entirely—was a sign to alert anybody? And those on her right were at some point released and now join in behind, scattering across the lanes like fire ants. Spokane: a city to be reckoned with.

She leans forward and peers, alert for funny business though her eyes glaze and the way ahead begins to resemble Turner's *Morning after the Deluge.* She makes a turn at Riverside, at Monroe, at Boone, each time slowing to scan traffic—which appears to have settled into the ordinary. She brings her shoulders back and down, encouraged but not willing yet to distract herself with the radio.

She is here to complete her studies.

On her trip through the cities and universities of the world, she has driven a number of cars, each one red. In the totemic arrangements of her native Pacific Northwest, red is the color of life; black, the spirit world. Her uncle Red died in Skagit County in a black Chevrolet sedan.

In the complex circuits of Haida and Kwakiutl mythology, in the earliest days all forms (raven, sun, man, bear, etc.) were interchangeable.[1]

She is not the one to say that this holds true, but here, sitting in her restored Rover TC 3500 on the Columbia Plateau—which sits on ancient lava flows as sublimely as a monkey tops a tree; as reliably as the pelvis balances on its femurs; as purposefully as a gargoyle hangs above the wall and spews water—she will guard her lane.

At Spokane the long, gradual slope from the Columbia River meets the sharp rise of the Rocky Mountain range. To the west, the desert-like Basin; east, the forested mountains of northern Idaho. She drives on a plateau, a transition area. Traveling with her, packed as neatly as possible, are the accumulations of travel, love and trouble, compressed by momentum and a backward glance as she crosses her home state in middle age. The change west to east is as beguiling as the transformation from Denmark to Palermo.

The rear-drive engine propels her gondola-style. Floating birds and ruffling animals visible at the roadside provide a lyricism found in the rococo. The renewing rivers and the recurrent theme of epiphany offer variety.

---

[1] Going up the coast, the Kwakiutl come before the Haida who come before the Tsimshian who come before the Inuit. The way to read a totem pole, on the other hand, is top down—all animals above except the bottom. Be sure to button up, the cold can pop your bones like a bullet.

Experience should be delicately balanced, endearing yet respectful, not at all pompous and only barely pious, and there may be the insertion of romantic, pastoral characters that later prove popular with landscape painters.

The familiar comprises the most foreign of influences, and though there is no vigilant guardian or guidepost surmounting this enterprise, she carries a portfolio of possibilities. After all, she'd read that a knight who, as a child, had been sold by his mother into slavery, ultimately regained his patrimony by marrying the King of Armenia's daughter.

And though one was not permitted to bear arms inside the old Mercato Nuovo of Florence, neither could one be arrested inside it for debt.

On the other hand, she is wary of slipping her feet into her high-top slippers for fear of what may be already inside.

And one day on Puget Sound, an even layer of clouds (such as composed her frequent companions) appeared to her to be marching down the sky at the same rate as the sun. A picture of the event resides in the glove box. It shows the muted sun and, below it, clouds perhaps "two fingers" deep, if one were measuring grey the way an old salt does the pending onset of night. Yet the line of sunlight that crosses the surface of the water—a straight line coming right at you, horizon to shore—is not broken by reflection of that cloudy gap.

All of this, of course, is correct in science and history; not so much in the registering of it. There are whole areas of thought to be worked out and some items—snack foods and hair products, for instance—may not be available in what seems to be a foreign country. She recorded the exact time of her departure and carries it with her. The world, after all, is wide open. One must step carefully not to fall out of it. She makes her notes.[2]

---

[2] The raven is north in all directions, protected since they acquired speech. The way to shoot people is side to side in a confined space like a gym. The coast is on the furthest edge left. Then north as fired pistols.

Architectural Details

She drives into the parking lot of the School of Architecture and Fine Design in her '67 red Volkswagen bug. At home, she knows, the quail will be lined up on the fence wondering if it is safe to drop down into the yard. Were she there, she'd answer them in one of the extant languages by keeping the cat inside and drawing the drapes. Here, however, the concern is less cat than capstone, more fence than feathers.

For coursework she diagrams the images she has seen. In this one the old walls remain, though there have been alterations to the core. Here, plinths—upon the upper moldings stand the columns and pilasters of shops which flank the bridge. Elsewhere, a single marble arch, the steps on the right leading to a shrouded entrance.

Another building is a fine specimen of the flamboyant, having most of its beauties of style and few of its faults. The tooth work on the side shows an effort to reconstruct the nave in the style of the choir and tower. The recesses are for the sick, laid there to be cured during the night by saints.[3]

Here the gabled arches increase in height and breadth

[3] The ionic foot and now its frieze: the dental arcade, a buccal pavilion, the echinus of abacus and colonnade supporting the entablature of sweet, sour, frisson; the alphabetical pilasters of precision, the lingual firing range—*majore,* and *minore,* maxilla, mangle, as things that are wrinkled and bare irretrievably pass by.

from side to center, the whole effect suggesting one great spreading porch of bays; though in this case so surrounded by high houses that only one portal can be seen. High up a circle has been carved that contains within it a painting of the sun. Images of trees, a shepherd and quizzical sheep appear to have been adapted from Catiglione's version of *The Flight*. She declaims Matthew Arnold at the entryway: "The sea is calm tonight, The tide is full, the moon lies fair Upon the Straits...."

The tail of the raven in flight is wedge-shaped, distinguishing it from the fan shape of the crow. A fantail is the stern overhang of a ship. Sometimes her mind is so full she must dismount and proceed on foot, supported by the angels.

Nothing so secret as sorrow.

Parts lying on the left and right banks of the Spokane River originally bore other names. The Natatorium has been replaced by a field of mobile homes. A false step here still thrills with fear.

A small section of one park was popularly called *Pentimento* after Pentti Karkiainen, cook's apprentice and lute player. Initially considered an oddity, he came to be regarded affectionately for his afternoon concerts in the garden. Resonance was heightened by his barely concealed sorrow for a life of misdeeds, the details of which were never fully revealed and, for all the listeners knew, may have been made up for effect—and anyway likely occurred in another country. The peculiar tuning of his instrument is still imitated.

Principles of Agriculture & Animal Science

She eases her burnt-red Pacer into the parking lot of the Ag School. Back in her apartment, she knows her cat is pacing and sleeping, alert and prepared at any moment to be completely indifferent at her return.

Thus far we have emphasized the importance of favorable conditions. Farmers may easily incorporate cooler days into the growing season by sowing early and may control moisture to a considerable extent by culture. A good oat will have as little as 30% hull and 70% or more kernel.

The experimental stations offer little evidence, but practically everyone agrees that fall plowing aids the distribution of labor. In leisure times, natural history and the study of comparative structures provide ample opportunity to regard the primrose, the insects that feed upon it, etc.[4] We know, for example, that fish, like humans, have the otolith, a dense calcific structure sometimes referred to as an "ear stone," a sensory organ that plays a role in hearing and balance.

The European Fish Ageing Network (EFAN) uses the

---

[4] Potato is the least dangerous crop; the most dangerous: tomato, for a long while. The poison of green, not yellow. Clothes stain, the necks of birds elongate. Wring the cloth. The way from sink to stove is wheel. Our hands are white, the box black, the sun rolls red beneath the lid.

otolith to age halibut, reading only those collected from the left or blind side. Halibut grow faster the farther north you go: a 40 lb fish off the coast of Washington is likely to be a lot older than a 40 lb fish off Kodiak.

The design of the eye of the raven on ceremonial posts is the face of another animal whose eye is the face of a yet smaller animal, whose own eye depicts an animal so tiny we are allowed only to sense it.

We may now turn to the consideration of the Hominoidea in some detail.

As night approaches, the gorilla builds a comfortable nest that it uses once then abandons. The lowland gorilla usually sleeps in trees, while mountain gorillas prefer the ground and occasionally a space under a rock ledge.

Gorillas are slow moving on ground and may be easily overtaken.

It happens again. Driving north on Lincoln the far left lane completely disappears and her own lane is forced to proceed in a direction she does not want to take at all.

Tillage is the greatest factor in setting soil foods free so plants and animals can use them. Soils are media, as are particular offices of the Diocese. Through intervention, elements are taken from the ground and returned to it. That the earth eventually yields up vast storehouses is a fortune taken on faith.

"Don't just be there," her old friends write in long, reminiscing letters from the coast. The hours sometimes pass like days in hospice. Her new friends say: "stay."

An oil painting purchased at auction reveals surprise

handwriting on the back: *I can see all the dinosaurs from Uncle Jim's ranch.* Humus is the life of the soil. Everything else is mystery.

The World of the Pharaohs; Paris, France

They are two couples and they've walked all day through Paris, foregoing the one bright red taxi that would carry the four of them. They lunch on rabbit paté in a stone tower, stop to look at painters near a bridge, and later, when it begins to drizzle, buy roasted nuts in paper bags.

Figures from Chapters 1 through 5:

Isometric reconstructions. Stone vessels shaped as baskets. The Blue Chambers, the Mortuary Complex, the Step Pyramid.

Now they are in Pigalle where they have wine and stroll through the wet, the posters and lights, the funneled music and evocative smells. Then they want to go to a skin show, all except David's wife who does not.

Figures from Chapter 6:

The Annointants clenching cylinders. Slab stela of Iuno with two opposing right hands, no left. Relative size of the sexes.

Djehuty-nakht seated, two opposing left hands. Papyrus thicket, donkey carrying sacks.

Kitchen scene: two left hands.

Four family members: right-left, one left-left, two right-right. Antef: two left. The sphinx, recumbent.

The nose of Amarna. Several subterranean courts with extensive branching corridors and shafts.

Two right.

The others are not much surprised at this refusal which does not, after all, greatly matter. They are not young; nothing can come as too much of a surprise. They will instead go back to the hotel for a nightcap.

Figures from Chapter 7:

View into an open canopic chest. Small string of faience beads. Pillars shaped like sistrums. The head of Hathor faces in all four directions, filling the great space with harmony.

Left-left.

The moment at which the priest stops and sets naos with its pillared plinth atop his foot. Not in fetters in this example.

On the way, the women have to go to the bathroom and are happy to find a sign on a stairway leading down under street level to the conveniences. They leave their husbands and wind down the acrid, spotty cement and to arrive at a large, bright, littered room with sinks and doors.

Figures from Chapter 8:

Amun as ram, recumbent. Shaft and false door; contact and transition. Giraffes symmetrical beside a palm. Here missing the ceiling and upper section of the walls.

The Queen's eyes made lifelike by rock crystal. With outstretched wings and shen rings in its claws, falcon's body returns each night to the tomb.

While they are checking to be sure they read the sign correctly—that it is a latrine for women not men—two strange men suddenly appear from the direction of the stairs behind them. Their hats are low on the foreheads, their shoulders bunched up toward their ears as if it were raining in the room, their hands are knotted and thrust deep into their pockets. They watch the women and lean toward them. The women turn to look with expressions that haven't had time yet to be this or the other.

Author's Supplemental Notes to Chapter 8 for the Second Edition:

A mild yet august expression. This bust does not reproduce the actual features.

A young girl removing a thorn from the foot of another. The cult building, beyond the courtyard. The kneeling ruler successively cleanses the baboon god, "The Great White One" with four containers of water; brings bolts of fabric to clothe the four-headed snake, "He Who Lives Through His Magic Power;" and worships the six-legged snake goddess, "She of The Nose."

A field of reeds.

By the time the women become frightened, but before they decide what to do, the husbands suddenly enter, having noticed the thugs descending and followed them. The Frenchmen register their arrival. One snarls.

Figures from Chapter 9:

The appearance of the god, falling down before the god, praising and offering gifts to the god, etc.

For awhile all six are as if arranged by a larger hand—silent, motionless, alert—while a variety of thoughts run through their minds. At last the intruders mutter something incomprehensible, brush by the husbands and go back up to the street.

Figures from Chapter 10:

A staggered arrangement, a turned head, a gesture, a leaning body. Here shown as a bull breaking through fortifications and trampling the enemy. The corners are animal heads, originally birds; in this example, hyenas.

The annual carrying up of images from the sanctuary to the temple roof to renew their powers with sunlight.

The husbands suggest getting out of there, which they quickly do, the women puzzled and compliant, accustomed to their men as professors and bankers rather than protectors and street fighters.

Figures from Chapters 11 through 14:

Winged sun-disk with Alexandrian garland, drape, cult figure of a falcon god, reminiscent of Pre-Dynastic dessications, on loan from the Bayerische Landesbank.

Not in Soleb but further south. Hittite prisoners. The emblematic "smiting of the foe:" a pile of severed penises. Small, iconographic deviations may be Persian.

One of these colossal statues is in the Louvre. The king triumphing over chaos, symbolized by dead animals. Two wives embrace his mummy, each wearing a white hairbag wig with her name on it. Copied inscriptions neglect to change the feminine form of "beloved" to the masculine.

A series of boat pits similar to later ship burials found in a Libyan city. Dragging the upper part of the statue to the Nile, then by ship from Alexandria to London.

As they walk in the direction of the hotel the women feel smaller than their escorts and keep close to them. They are unsure and full of questions and surmises and use their hands too much when they speak. The men are quiet, distracted, tall, irritable, proud, distant.

Figures from Chapter 15:

The ideal of the totality of space (4, the totality of the four cardinal points with the absolute multiplicity of all life forms; 3, being the plural of things and beings; 9 the plural of the plural and thus the totality of all forms and variations.)

A land identified by papyrus.

The statement that the obelisks were "covered with electrum along their entire length" may be taken as exaggeration.

Left-left.

Drinks in the bar do not inspire or calm them and they retire abruptly to their rooms with muttered reminders of the early bus to the Rodin Museum and Napoleon's Tomb.

They only have a handful of hours. They sleep fitfully, thoughtful in their hard beds.

The dead god-king holds his crook and flail.

Mineralization

Silicates of the serpentine group may be a shade of green so common in nature that from a distance, through a lens, they are taken for low, stiff plants. Varieties have separate elastic fibers suitable for soundproofing and insulation. Others are opaque or of a pearly luster. Some fuse with difficulty or are, in fact, infusible.

A crust under force forms corrugations, prominences, hollows. Monuments of the desert valley leak calcium and are drilled by wind. Sections of exposed ridge on canyon walls are either empty arches or what is left when folds below die out. The bones of her aging neck turn to stone, her family to dust. She buys silk to warm a fusing core and slow the heat that senses the freedom of the outside and flies toward it.

She seeks another place to live, pairing change with silence, the latter no longer socially prized. In the sculpture of discard, above the architrave, the marble bride tightens. Her accumulations are not easily released; nor the small, carved bouquet. Life wants to reverberate. A charge arcs to circuit—first as strong, then pale arm. The assumption that nature will preserve its slower, sweeter shapes is deleted in the edits.

The Patient Bearing of Trials

Maybe, the Jesuit said, Heaven is an instant. That white light.

Every tree, a nest—but for the sake of clarity we must return to the tuning of stringed instruments.

Amplitude carries. Intensity is a ratio. The amount of energy per unit time is power. She often listens to gavottes and tarantellas while preparing dinner but switches to something more cello for the meal.

How sound in water differs from sound in air: The wave spreads out and gets smaller as some is absorbed by seawater. Absorption depends on frequency and at certain decibels the spirit is pulled from the body, out and up in a spiral that tugs at the chest with increasing pressure. Roots are ripped from their soil; skirts torn free from the doorway where they caught while passing through. A beak tears relentlessly, one good part from another and there is no sadness like a feather lost; a wing one.

Right hand or left, one should hold on to something.

Primitive clavichords possessed only the diatonic scale of C. Tuning was accomplished by commas. Known as unequal temperament, this method suits a simple scale and pieces with scant modulation. All systems over time undergo change.

Her neighbors are listening to a cover of "Land of Confusion" by Disturbed, whose tuning has all strings down 1/2 half step. Her own reserves, depleted by wakefulness, are restored online by auctions: watercolors of Whidbey Island, the Olympic Peninsula, the California coast; an Inuit stone carving of a breaching whale; agates and shark's teeth. Every nest, a tree[5].

She tries sleeping on the opposite side of the bed. As if study was an end in itself.

And, among the withering rock faces of a gorge, she examines whether some thoughts might add to us in ways that do not move us forward; whether we may be diminished, whether we know what forward is, whether thought is not sometimes a thing.[6]

So far we have discussed various systems for approaching the relentless turn of the seasons.

Machines that increase efficiency—the gang plow, section harrow, corn cultivator, thresher, huller, etc.—power the muscles of the day, but nothing, for those wakeful in the stilled, discomfiting night, speeds the hands of a clock along in darkness from one safe number to the next.

No musical sound is isolate but is accompanied by harmonics.

---

[5] Name the circulation system. A bird believes the place it lives—the wood-barn; the sunned plank. Circumnavigated, wrecked, and then suddenly "Professor of Natural History and Modern Languages." Each spring a glorious plume, a loosed hornet, a noosed reed.

[6] To cover a wall with paintings, put darker at the bottom, lighter high: anchor, sky. Some jogged, some dipped, aside. There are horizons. Dagger the walls. The Sparrow Hawk left, the Grey Fox right. A hammer for the Pigeon. Everyone carry something.

At the mouth of a river we know that sea and fresh water mix, but so slowly that the latter, muddy and discolored, floats for a time above the salt. The wake of passing vessels reveals lines of blue mingling in little eddies. The universe conflates and exhales; some parts falling, some holding on.

The word spinet derives from a kind of spine used to pluck the strings; or from Spinetus, the probable inventor of the instrument—either source rooted in the idea of columnar structures to flexibly enforce the whole. Complete the following exercises:

(1) Locate the Isaac Stevens School, a handsomely painted Colonial Revival building supporting its gable with four ionic columns.

(2) Navigate the south edge of Fairhaven where Twelfth Street bends to become Chuckanut Drive.

The oversized map of Seattle, 1889, is suitable reference though a reprint from 1946.

By now Lytton Strachey has complained in a letter to Virginia Woolf that there are times when he seems to see life steadily and see it whole but these are only moments and, as a rule, he can make nothing out.

Virginia has, by turn, answered: "One flies into the air. Next time, I mean to stick closer to facts."

Ravens hover in place like kestrels, soar like hawks.[7] Each day she drives *Out of the light and mutely*.[8]

The beads are wood and black, but is not the figure on the medallion too thin?

She requires an occasional dip into Irving's account of the fur trade, 1836—"They…were ready to do and suffer any thing for the good of the enterprise." She believes that if she could accurately identify the keys of stress, she might resolve them in a lower major.

Her collections have grown to include a segment of columnar basalt shaped like a bird bath; a cup with a map of the Inside Passage; a brass counterweight marked "1000 grm." The row of evergreens planted in autumn clearly aspires, but may never become tall. She frames her pictures and hangs every one; saves interesting cones in a Marsh Wheeling cigar box—acquiring tidiness the way a bird finds twigs.

She has lost some things, too: Aunt Rose's coin purse, Uncle Red's ring. The dead will have their mementos.

~

White, red and black war shields in the archipelago are passed from generation to generation, each hand-over marking the same painful change.

Drainage systems in mountainous areas branch and

---

[7] I shudder anymore, wherever grows an angle. How one now reads past needs, the heart in the chair, the leg numb by the fire, the lamp against an obelisk of cold that spreads down, down and inward. I shudder some, anymore, most of the time.

[8] Matthew Arnold

dwindle like veins of the body—sightless but always reaching toward something. The pattern holds true in the flats.

More secretive than anyone, JMW Turner had a strong instinct for painting as performance and was generally one of the first to arrive at the Royal Academy, coming down before breakfast and continuing his labor as long as daylight lasted.

Robert Leslie remarked: "Besides red-lead, he had a blue which...tempered with crimson or scarlet...he worked over his near waters in the darker lanes."

When Augustus Wall Callcott was asked what Turner was doing, he said: "I should be sorry to be the man to ask him."

She purchases cloth ginkgo panels in a flower-and-pot store, thinking how to adapt them for stained glass. She worries that if she doesn't buy a thing when she sees it she will never encounter it again—a vexation common among the religious—and so is always acting on what she sees; though closing her eyes tight at an overhang of rock.[9]

---

[9] "The Mango Pots of Veuve (The Widow) Rantala"
The spider has for circuit, foreshortened.

Webbed mangoes,
crushed considerations of flush trees.

Everyday like this

pots abiding the abodes of hiss

strange champagnes
drown the lucky snake
in his.

Everyday a beading rain.

~

Spokane is a grid, unlike the spidery, twisted warrens of old Seattle, but moves mostly north and south, the river taking the east-west burden. What she drives now is burgundy and has hardly any mileage compared to her own. Sometimes she jumps right up for no reason at all in the middle of something else to get in the car and drive around—it is an old habit, quadruped not biped the natural order of things—though the formulaic layout of the town makes discovery unsatisfying: she always ends up where predicted, even if the lanes taking her there seem capricious. And when she gets there someone always feels compelled to speak.

She prefers the Palouse, the vast quilt of farms and hollows that rolls out from the edge of town to cover the south and east. Roads meander through it by weaves, dips and mounds, now turning for barns and pieces of towns, now for creeks and silos—each rise opening to a vista of startling beauty.

The colors of the earth (for there are few trees) mark the time of year—honey golds and greens, yellows, oranges, dark browns stiff with white frost. It is possible that color is its beating heart and one can be alone in it.

She has seen such paintings in her life: a red skiff; a lifting tern; waves of frozen groundcover sparkling like an undulate sea.

Distance in the Palouse is stark and soft. The reach goes farther and farther from the eye; nothing new in it but the wind. It could be that those old silt dunes stretch so far that they outpace the soul.

When she would stand in the rain forests of the Pacific Northwest, the wet reflections always turned her inward.

Here, in these vast rolling fields, a part of her self wanders out of sight. She hopes to retrieve it before the snow.

In the Canopy

I have misled you.
You stand at the foot of a mountain
It is winter

You try to peer through the branches

Paavo Haavikko,
from "The Bowmen,"
translated by Anselm Hollo

"Listen, this sounds like Paganini," she said, looking over to him but nodding toward the sound system; and he said quickly, pleasantly, carefully, "no, it sounds like Accardo *playing* Paganini." She laughed brightly, "Yes, it is."

~

An eagle slipping soundlessly over the neighbor's house spotted their cat in the back yard and changed direction to come down for it. It was so big and low it confused her from the deck. "Look!" she said to her husband and pointed, "Is that an eagle?"

Her voice caught the attention of the eagle which turned its head in their direction. It slowed almost to a hover, hanging there, factoring. Then, it pushed its big wings down in a dramatic, dignified kind of way and pulled them slowly back up again, angling back around and sort of loping along on its original path.

~

They were snooping through a box of his aunt's letters. Sometimes his eye went on its own to the lid, cast onto its back like a turtle, but her enthusiasm had a greater force than his guilt.

"I think this one's from a student," she whispered, placing a hand on his arm. "Listen."

"Mary Hamilton Swindler's book, 'Ancient Painting: From the Earliest Times to the Period of Christian Art,' [blah, blah, blah]. *Anyway, the book made me think of sending this to you.*

"Then there's this long poem. Ha! Take a look."
He read:

"Evolution"

More to go
and no ideas yet,
even now, adrift in the canopy
as we send ourselves out
piece by piece to sleep,
with no idea yet of where to go
or how we will know it
and how we will look to ourselves
when we get there.
We sift quietly,
smaller and smaller fragments,
little by littling,
death in sleep.
Unsorted from the beginning,
a loose, unlikely momentum.

Even in a place
so familiar that we imagine home,
but not like the only one we'll ever have,
and even when the skin around us and the next
rub companionably in the blue, cool air
as a leaf and tree might
when one of them moves.

More to go even then
and nothing foreseen.
More
or maybe not more,
something.
Something perhaps wanted.
A want without desire.
As something in a tree
wants a field.

"From art to monkeys," he said. "I guess that makes sense. Lord knows the reverse is true!"

They were laughing when they heard tires crunch the gravel in the drive. Quickly, they put the letter back in the envelope, the envelopes back in the box, the lid back on top and the box itself back on the closet shelf.

~

She told him a story:

Once there were two sisters. One of them wore herself outside in, the other, inside out. In all other ways except age, they were alike, as much as sisters can be alike, which is both a lot and not at all.

The one sister let everything she saw come in. She took everything in from outside. One day she said: Today I am going to learn Greek; and she did. Another day she said: I am going to be a classical musician. Sometimes she just took things in without comment: she bought a car; she had a baby. She didn't mention everything. Not, for instance, if she didn't think she was going to keep it very long.

The other sister took everything in, too, but could not use it in any practical way. So everything she took in she thought about, then looked for something she could have that seemed like it. She wore herself inside out. Soon she had a room filled with things she'd taken in and taken out again: crackled icons; miniature amphorae; a machine to play the records she bought after hearing beautiful things. Things from watching her sister and things that had nothing to do with her at all: a beautifully bound book of poems; a mouse.

Sometimes the sisters tried each other out. That is, they each tried the reverse. It didn't work very well. One would not take care of her things. The other found she could not speak. Each way required its special skills.

Once they tried just to be more like the other. At the end of the day they were halfway this, halfway that. Then they were frightened it might take both of them to make one. Then they were afraid there would be no one left to be a sister to. And then they were afraid they would die.

One day, one of them did die. The outside-in one. She was lying in her bed thinking how she should go about dying, and then she did. The other one could not believe it and stared for a long time without moving or breathing. The doctor looked at the bed and said: "She's gone."

A minute or two later the inside-out one, who had been quite still, suddenly took a very deep breath. This alarmed the doctor who turned to look at her. But, as nothing further happened, he left.

When she also left the room she was just her. She didn't know exactly what to do. She had taken in something, but could not use it in any practical way. And then she was afraid she would die. And then she was afraid she would not.

~

When he was alone, he sometimes saw something like what looked like a deep hole floating in the step, or in the foyer, or among the clustered asters at the front. It appeared in many places and when he saw it he would stop and look at it. Sometimes he would feel a small sort of engine start in him.

At those times he thought the best thing for him was to stay where he was and keep looking. Then it might also happen that he would also see a ripple or a fish, in which case he would look for tackle; he would reach for the rudder, feel for scales.

When he was alone he sometimes stopped and looked, approaching happiness and staying with it awhile—on a porch, in a room, on a beach or jetty or bank, and in a boat, one hand on the motor, one attached to line.

~

Her grandfather played the cello and her aunt was a concert pianist. "I come from a musical family," she would say in conversation.

She told her aunt, one afternoon in the living room, "I wish I'd learned an instrument. It must be thrilling to be in the middle of an orchestra with all that sound coming at you from all directions."

"Yes," the aunt agreed, "it is wonderful."

"I wish I had, I really do," she went on dreamily. "Maybe an oboe or French horn." She paused. "But I'd probably make a mistake at a noticeable time."

"Yes," the aunt said. "There's that."

~

One year a storm hit the city and was later named for the holiday on which it fell.

They improvised their dinners because the power had gone out and talked into the evening by the fireplace because there was no TV or light to read by and because they were excited and did not know what to expect.

When they had tired of talking, they opened up a bottle of red wine. Leaves, branches and paper blew all over the neighborhood, piling up against the fences and porches and into the drains, stopping them up. Shingles came loose, rain leaked onto sills, trees fell. Animals hid and shivered and some ran away.

One other year, in the distant past, on that very same day, a man had stood beside Columbus at the prow of a skiff. He saw the sun, the shore, the landing spot, the faces watching them from between the leaves. He balanced on his two mortal feet, framed by sky and sea, and hoped there would not be any trouble.

~

When her aunt was dying, they took her with them to

the coast, to a literary hotel and checked her into the Hemingway room. She would rather have been in the Woolf Room or the Nin or Colette room, or in a musical hotel, but that weekend they took what they could get.

Curled horns hung above her bed and the zebra-striped bedspread, but when they went down to dinner they ate like city people, like rich Parisians: pâté and crackers, champagne, roasted duck; although by this time she didn't eat very much.

A poet once lived in the room before it had been decorated for authors, when it was room 102 of a rundown building in Newport. He'd hung his long, brown coat over the window to block out the sun and the sounds of the beach, the people, the birds, the waves—everything that moved, sounded or shone—so he could write.

She hadn't heard of this poet, but was grateful for the soft bed and a room that didn't look like any she had been in before.

~

He had been staring into his coffee when she noticed he was also smiling. He was happiest when he had a plan.

It would be a good book or a monograph," he said. "*Flat Feet*. It would draw connections between Watson's book, *Darwin: The Indelible Stamp,* and people's understanding of human anatomy; how to interpret the 'scars of human evolution,' you know, the very non-useful things we have inherited like weak backs, tailbones and flat feet."

It was Saturday morning and a fine, dense Seattle mist

clung to the windows. While he continued to think, she listened to Brahms' Third Symphony on the radio. As the second movement was giving way to the third, the mist began to accumulate into drops and merge together with other drops and as they grew heavier and bigger and more complex they sagged and ran down the glass in wavy wet lines making a kind of curtain.

~

"Hey! "Look at that!" she said to him as the train rocked her against a seatback.

"I actually met her once in New York," he replied.

She put the newspaper clipping of Uta Hagen in her wallet against a picture of her aunt. Where it had been, where she'd found it, it had made a dark stain of itself on the title page of *Primitive Heritage* by Mead and Calas. It was a new, used book. They were traveling by train, for two days already, and she hadn't noticed the clipping before then.

"Hey!" she'd said to him, when she was taking it out the book, and again to the person in the next row of seats, "look at that! Uta Hagen!"

"And, he met her!" she said to the next person.

~

He told her a story of himself:

I had been looking where you had never been, in the megaliths and the bronze burial fields where water kept the dead in a kind of circus, floating and held down, continuous for centuries as for a day.

The fields ran excited in the same direction as our bus, tossing like pale manes; as assured of themselves as all the recently shorn are of their comeliness. We were a view of nothing and they would not miss us.

Later the forest came close and dark as sockets but for a narrowed light that dropped down and lit us like the hearth of a cabin we might not want to enter. In the deep: a dip in middle. A man who had said nothing all day pointed to the swamp, a green choke of drained sea.

We few on the bus were a body behind its master. Trees counted us easily on their green thumbs, ignoring the man who turned emptily toward the one who had left him, as well as the woman at the kiosk dragging an empty sweater by one arm.

Then, there were chalk white cliffs where the dust climbed into our clothes and ears. We thought we could not run so fast to be so high. A boy collected flint. The swans and gulls veered from sea toward a sharper color and disappeared.

Then, we went down, down beneath a tardy moon. The trees leaned—willows, oaks, the scrubs we have at home, a small red berry. The bus worked along an edge we could not watch and later I heard shoes scrape on a mat. Then I fell hard asleep against a glass.

It was an excursion we thought might end us. "Better keep together," the guide said. Our wheels leapt again onto the hard road, our shades jumping on the farms, the animals, the rust, and right in front of me a man who had been sleeping smoothed his hair. His nails left a thin trail on his skin. I was afraid they would go through. His hand tightened when I told him about the birds.

Out of the air again and into town. There was an old church, but I was out of film. A woman lost her keys. Near a fence a horse lay all the way down on its side.

It was our longest day in our way of doing nothing, and though I did not know I was looking, I knew that I hadn't found you. We had a stone, a flint, and a schedule, and time passed. To everything we had eclipsed that day we must have seemed to have had wings.

~

When her uncle died, they gave his horse, Pal, to a man named Albert — who all their lives had lived in Cedar City raising pedigreed boxer dogs, but who last year moved out of town and high up into Cedar Breaks because of the throwback black puppies he was not supposed to keep but wouldn't kill just because they were not brown. Pal and the puppies would share a barn and corral that had once been a set for a movie, a Western with Randolph Scott. There was a meadow there with grass and fine aspens and a brook and many, many birds and it didn't look anything like Utah at all.

~

"When I come back," the neighbor said, putting his wine glass down carefully, "I'm coming back as a bird."

"Don't fly over me," his wife shrieked.

"I saw a cartoon in the New Yorker," another woman

said, "where an angel with a clipboard came up to a soul ensconced in the clouds and told him in a shipboard-activity-director sort of way that there were openings for reincarnation and he could sign up for either a mongoose or a wombat." The wife shrieked again.

"And you," the neighbor said, in an equally jovial tone to the woman and her husband," you'll probably both want to come back as monkeys."

"No," her husband offered for both of them, "you just don't know about primates. It might be better to come back as a cat. A cat is clearly what it is. No one expects it to be anything else. Being able to hide at the drop of a hat wouldn't be all bad either."

~

One day he told her a story of them:

Two visitors to Padua were having a hard time breathing and sleeping in the dusty city. Mopeds, smokers, diesels and tiny, frequent cars whose occupants leaned and waved and honked and whistled, all combined with the heat, the aging buildings and wood shutters to make everything penetrable, gritty and clouded up; dust covered dust.

On weekends their host, sensing their struggle, took them to the hills, to the tall pines and hydrangea-rimmed gardens, the villas, the olive trees, the green measurable spaces between guests. There they were soothed by the shiny dark wood floors of the hotel, the white starched linens and curtains that made them feel as if they were in an elegant hospital. Inhaling deeply, they flopped onto the low beds and stretched their arms. *Ah, Italia!* they breathed, embracing the privileged mountains of patronage.

Those mornings, they dressed and joined their host downstairs for breakfast. They chose thick, dark coffee and hard crusted bread and smooth butter and golden cheeses and chilled juice and brilliant eggs with tissue-thin slices of ham and colorful chunks of fruit. They ate and talked of the fine beds and, afterward, strolled in the gardens and wore their jackets on their shoulders as they had seen locals do, and clasped their hands behind their backs like Continentals.

Soon they were driven back to their apartment to continue the lectures to students and cough themselves to sleep. They did not say much to their friends about the old city, beautiful though it was, but in their letters home the travelers described the smallest details of the hotel, the clouds, the enormous blue flowers, the spires of dark trees, the moments of blissful forgetfulness; though their friends all along had imagined them there and only there; rested, jackets draped on their shoulders, happy in the quiet groves, the morning mists, the hills, the airy land.

~

"I'm sure it's not time yet," she said to him the morning of the funeral, after waking suddenly and checking her watch by the bedside light.

"See? Too early," she said and turned off the lamp.

"Plenty of time," she assured him; adding, though he did not respond, "don't worry." She fluttered a hand vaguely in his direction and settled her head back into the bowl she'd made of the pillow. "Way, way too soon."

About Kathryn Rantala

Kathryn Rantala's fiction and poetry have appeared in *The Denver Quarterly, Field, Iowa Review, Archipelago, Painted Bride Quarterly,* and many other places since 1974. She is the author of "Traveling With the Primates" (2008), "The Plant Waterer and other things in common" (2006), "Missing Pieces, a coroner's companion" (1999), and two chapbooks, "As If They Were a Basket" (2008) and "The Dark Man" (1975). She founded *Ravenna Press* (ravennapress.com), *Snow Monkey* and *The Anemone Sidecar.*

Recent Books by Casa de Snapdragon

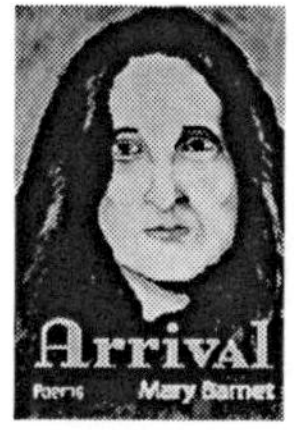

Arrival
Mary Barnet
Illustrated by
Richard E. Schiff
978-0-9840530-8-7f
Poetry

Storiana
Penelope Weiss
978-0-984053-06-3
Short Stories

Water under Water
Charles Adés Fishman
978-0-9840530-2-5
Poetry

The Making of Tibias Ivory
Through the Eyes of Innocence
D. Allen Jenkins
978-0-9840530-4-9
Relationships, Prejudice

Spectral Freedom
Select Poetry, Criticism, and Prose
Lynn Stongin
Poetry, Short Stories

A Scattering of Imperfections
Katrina K Guarascio
978-0-9793075-8-4
Poetry

Harriet Murphy
A Little Bit of Something
Janet K. Brennan
978-0-9793075-6-0
Short Stories

I Found My Father in a Women's Prison
Tracey Brown, PhD
978-0-9793075-3-9
Christianity, Poetry

Visit https://www.casadesnapdragon.com for information on these and other books.

LaVergne, TN USA
04 November 2010
203567LV00004B/67/P

9 780984 053094